Second Home

Also by Margaret Rodeheaver

Hidden Treasure (Chinkapin Series Book 1)
Finders Keepers (Chinkapin Series Book 2)

Children's books by M. M. Rodeheaver

Porkington Hamm
Porkington Returns
Haunted Holiday - A Christmas Cookie Ghost Story

Second Home

Chinkapin Series Book 3

Margaret Rodeheaver

Pares Forma Press

MACON, GEORGIA

Pares Forma Press/Will Way Books, Inc.
212 Will Way
Byron, Georgia 31008
www.MargaretRodeheaver.com

Publisher's Note: This is a work of fiction. Names, characters, places, and
incidents are a product of the author's imagination or are used fictitious-
ly. Locales and public names are sometimes used for atmospheric purposes. Any resemblance to actual people, living or dead, or to businesses,
companies, events, institutions, or locales is completely coincidental.

Book Layout ©2017 BookDesignTemplates.com
Cover design by Rebecacovers

Ordering Information:
Quantity sales. Special discounts are available on quantity purchases by
bookstores, associations, libraries, and others. For details, contact Will
Way Books, Inc. at the address above.

Second Home/ Margaret Rodeheaver. -- 1st ed.
Print ISBN 978-1-7332880-2-6
Large Print ISBN 978-1-7332880-6-4
EBook ISBN 978-1-7332880-3-3

"Clothe yourselves with compassion, kindness, humility, gentleness and patience... And over all these virtues put on love, which binds them all together."

Contents

Chapter 1...1

Chapter 2..13

Chapter 3..23

Chapter 4..33

Chapter 5..47

Chapter 6..57

Chapter 7..75

Chapter 8..87

Chapter 9..97

Chapter 10. 111

Chapter 11. 119

Chapter 12. 135

Chapter 13. 153

Chapter 14. 171

Chapter 15. 185

Chapter 16. 197

Chapter 17. 211

Chapter 18. 227

Chapter 19.. 237

Chapter 20.. 247

Chapter 21.. 263

Chapter 22.. 275

Chapter 23.. 287

Chapter 24.. 303

Chapter 25.. 313

Chapter 26.. 325

Chapter 1.

Laurie Lanton had finally made it to the big leagues. She was one of the cool girls; a member of the "in" crowd.

She had her own key to the Treasure Chest.

Looking over her shoulder at the overcast sky, Laurie unlocked the door to the thrift shop and wrestled it open against the December wind. It thudded shut behind her, bells jangling on the glass. She shrugged off her jacket in the office and walked through the shop switching on lights.

At the end of the hall she plugged in the artificial tree and lingered to examine all the Christmas items the shop offered for sale. Among the ornaments, wreaths, coffee mugs, and everything else celebrating the winter holidays, a collection of snowmen caught her eye. She bunched them together with some Christmas ornaments and greenery, returned to the office for her cellphone, and took several pictures for a Facebook post, hoping to entice customers to come buy the items before they went on sale for half price.

The bells jangled again against the door, and Laurie walked to the front of the shop to find Mary smoothing her hair into place. "Ooh, I wish that wind would lay," she said.

"It probably will, whenever it starts raining," Laurie said. "There's a sixty percent chance by noon today."

Mary hung her jacket next to Laurie's and surveyed her friend approvingly. "Look at that cute top you have on! Did you buy it here?"

Laurie wore an electric blue drape-y tunic spangled with sequins over a pair of skinny jeans. She gave her brown locks a toss. "No, for a change. I bought this new when Chase and I were up visiting his family for Thanksgiving. Every now and then I have to remind myself why I hate shopping on Black Friday." She grimaced. "But it gave us something to do with his brother and sister-in-law."

Mary nodded. All the volunteers at the Treasure Chest were good customers of the shop, and on any given day at least a few of them were dressed in donated clothing. They certainly found plenty of interesting items to buy. Mary especially could not resist baby clothes for Ricky, her eight-month-old. "Did you put the cash in the drawer yet?" she asked.

"Just got the lights in the back switched on. I'll get the rest, and check the thermostat while you get the money."

Mary fetched the cash kept on hand for openers, and counted it into the drawer. "It looks cozy in here today," she said, gathering up the one dollar bills and beginning her count again.

"Good thing, because it's awfully gloomy outside!" Despite the dust and clutter, the shop did look cozy. Laurie was fond of the place. It had been something of a refuge for her, after she divorced DB and moved south to start life over in a warmer climate and a little closer to her best friend Mary, who she had known since forever.

Mary slid the cash drawer closed and folded her arms. "And I feel gloomy, knowing that Don is coming in this morning with all of Alice's stuff."

"I know," Laurie agreed. "The funeral was just ... what? Two weeks ago?"

"I imagine he wants to get it done while his kids are still in town to help go through everything. It's not just the timing, though. Alice was the person who trained me." Laurie smiled at the thought, and Mary smiled too. "Well, as much training as it takes to work here, but seriously. She showed me the ropes, and was so friendly and encouraging. She always made me feel special."

"That's how Alice made everyone feel. Poor Don. It's going to be an adjustment for him, for sure."

Mary went to the staff kitchen, flipped through a few disks, and put some lively Christmas music on the old CD player. "Maybe this will perk us up," she said. "Life is short. I feel like I should get out and do something fun and crazy and reckless while I still can."

"What did you have in mind?" Laurie asked raising her eyebrows suggestively. Mary and her husband Pete both struck her as fairly conservative, in a progressive sort of way.

"I know, right? We're so stodgy lately, crazy and reckless would be drinking black coffee after eight o'clock at night."

"I kind of think I'm acting crazy and reckless getting married again and buying a house," Laurie said. She didn't really mean it, though. She was sure about Chase Harris. *Sure* sure. And she knew that Chase was sure about her. After all, this wasn't their first rodeo, for either of them.

"Speaking of married, where's that ring, girlfriend?" Mary grabbed Laurie's hand and let it drop to the counter again. "I thought you'd have one by now."

"Hey, the day's not over! We've been looking around. I just haven't seen anything that speaks to me yet. Plus I'm cheap. Part of me wants to skip the diamond engagement ring, although I wished I'd had one Thanksgiving weekend. I swear, every time we told one of Chase's relatives that we were getting married I saw them glance at my left hand. Made me want to wear gloves! When I leave here today Chase and I are going to check out the pawn shop. Hard to believe I've lived next door to it for almost a year and still haven't been inside."

Laurie and Chase had both been short of funds when they'd moved to Chinkapin, and likely were lured in by the same apartment ad: "Efficient and affordable. Convenient to downtown Chinkapin and the interstate." It wasn't a lie. But there wasn't much else to recommend the little complex next to the Chinkapin pawn shop where each had a one-bedroom apartment.

Mary glanced out the glass door and tipped her head in the direction of the parking lot. "Speaking of marriage, here comes Don." Laurie walked around the counter and held the door open.

A tall, silver-haired man walked through carrying a large cardboard box. "Purses and shoes," he said briskly. "Where would you like them?"

"Come on to the tagging room." Mary led the way to one of the back rooms where space had been made to receive Alice's belongings.

Laurie pushed the door open again for Alice's daughter. "Hello, Charlotte. It's good to see you." Laurie made a point of being friendly to the attractive middle-aged blonde, who had commissioned Chase to write a song for Alice's funeral.

"Hey, Laurie. These are full of jewelry." Charlotte indicated the two flat boxes she carried.

"I'll take them," Laurie said. "We'll tag these here in the office, and probably put some of the items in the display case." She set the boxes on the counter and looked sympathetically at Charlotte. "This must be so hard for you."

"Well..." Charlotte unzipped her jacket and looked slowly around the shop, and then back at Laurie. "It is and it isn't. God bless her, Mom did everything she could to prepare us for this. She knew her prognosis, even before the accident. She'd been sorting through her things little by little, and already gave the important ones away to us kids. The stuff that I've brought you is pretty, but it's just costume jewelry. Some of it is a little out of style but, you know, hold on to it long enough and it'll be in again!"

"Your mother was a beautiful woman. Always dressed so sharp. And she was so kind to everyone. We sure do miss her around here."

Charlotte nodded. Don headed back to the car for another box, and Charlotte followed. "He looks better than he did at the funeral," Laurie said to Mary.

"He does. More like himself again. Lord, look at all that stuff." Mary held open the door as Don and Charlotte trudged through with armloads of blouses, slacks, and jackets, all on hangers. Mary relieved Charlotte of her items and followed Don to the back room. Laurie and Charlotte went out for another load.

Finally Don sat in the chair across from the counter. "There's one more box full of lingerie," Charlotte said. "I'll be right back." She pushed the door open and a gust of cold, damp air blew in.

The cheery music pouring from the CD player suddenly seemed inappropriate. Mary went to turn it down. Laurie didn't know quite what to say to Don. "Is there much more at home?" she asked finally.

"No, this is about it. Charlotte kept some of her mother's things for herself, and weeded out some that weren't worth bringing in. I hated seeing Alice's clothes in the drawers and closets, knowing she would never be back for them, but I'm not sure I like the empty spaces any better." He met Laurie's gaze with a wan smile.

"How about plans for the future. You're staying in Chinkapin, aren't you?"

"Oh, I don't think it's smart to make any changes in a hurry, although my son in North Carolina has been after me to move up that way. We'll see. I do understand the advantages of having family nearby, and I have no one left in Georgia. Charlotte has been a big help to me. I would have hated doing this by myself." He stood, and glanced across the parking lot at St. Mark's Episcopal Church. "Is the reverend next door this morning? I wanted to stop and see Barbara, but I can wait until tomorrow."

Laurie glanced through the office window. "That's her car, out behind the church."

"I'll just go over and speak to her for a minute." He held the door as Charlotte came in with the last box. "I'll be right back," he told her.

Charlotte set the box on the counter with a thump. "Here you go. I found several things that still have the tags on them, and some others that are barely worn."

"We do appreciate it," Laurie said.

"It's what Mom wanted us to do. In fact," Charlotte interrupted herself with a laugh, "she put it in writing. 'Keep whatever you want, and take the rest to the Treasure Chest.' Mom really loved this place." She sat in the chair her step-father had just left. "I'm exhausted."

"You deserve a vacation after all this."

"I'm driving back to Alabama tomorrow. I already let them know I will not be in to work until Tuesday. Thank God for substitute teachers." She smiled. "But you're right. I'm looking forward to staying home and doing nothing over Christmas break. It's been hard dealing with my own loss and also with Don's. He really, really loved her. He looks tough on the outside, but he's a marshmallow on the inside." She nodded to herself. "He's a good man."

* * *

By noon Laurie's travel mug was empty and her stomach had started to growl. Just as she looked up at the clock, the bells on the shop door jangled and Chase entered with her lunch and coffee. "Aren't you a sight for sore eyes," she said, diving for the bag in his hands.

"Do you mean me or the sandwich?" he asked, dangling it just out of reach.

Laurie looked at his angular face. Chase wasn't what you would call classically handsome, but the warmth of his smile made him very appealing. He wore a blue double-breasted wool jacket with the collar turned up, which reminded Laurie of an old-time navy recruiting poster. The jacket showed off his strong shoulders and trim waist.

She put her arms around him and gave him a hug. "You *and* the sandwich. But ooh, you feel cold! Take that jacket off and sit with me while I eat." She led him by the hand into the office.

"How's it going today?" he asked.

"Not bad. Selling quite a few Christmas things. I guess my ad worked."

"Don't sprain your shoulder patting yourself on the back," Mary said, leaning over to toss a plastic hanger into the box under the counter. "Hey, where's *my* sandwich? Don't tell me I have to eat the nasty leftovers I brought. Speaking of which, I need to throw them in the microwave." She wandered back into the staff kitchen and tinkered with the CD player while her food warmed.

"You're here until 2:00, right?" Chase asked, watching Laurie dig into her sandwich.

"Yep. Or a little after, depending on how long it takes us to cash out."

"Where'd all this stuff come from?" He looked around at all the jewelry spread out on the desk.

"It was Alice's. And this is just the tip of the iceberg. You should see the clothes and shoes and things in the back room. It's sad," Laurie said, "sorting through things we all remember her wearing to church just a few months ago, deciding whether to put four- or five-dollar price tags on them." The sandwich was momentarily forgotten.

"Think of how happy it'll make someone. Think of the money you'll be able to give to the food bank. Think of what stuff like this meant to us when we were starting over."

Laurie leaned her head on Chase's shoulder, feeling comforted. "You haven't found any diamond engagement rings in there, have you?" he asked.

She pulled her head away and gave him a squinty-eyed glance. "Ha-ha. No."

"Hey, you're the one who wants to go look in the pawn shop today. Where do you think that stuff comes from? Dead people, people who split up and didn't want to keep a nasty old ring from some dirtbag." He stopped suddenly, and looked sheepishly at Laurie. "Sorry."

She swallowed and picked at her sandwich, not meeting his eyes. Chase knew Laurie always referred to her ex by his actual initials, DB, although these days she usually meant "dirtbag."

"Whatever. Maybe I don't need an engagement ring," she said. Then she brightened. "Come to think of it, I still have my old rings. Maybe I can work out an exchange with the pawn shop."

"Worth a try," Chase agreed. "We'll find you something nice soon. Don't let my stupid remark stop you from getting something you want."

"Oh, I won't, Chase Harris. You're buying me a ring, all right. And I plan to flaunt it. No one has to know where it comes from."

"Yes, ma'am," he said, glad to see her look more cheerful. "I'm going to get out of here before I put my foot in it again."

Chapter 2.

The two women finished their lunch, and then rummaged through clothes in the back room in between waiting on customers. "It's jam-packed in here," Mary said. "I think we should put out every last coat and jacket that's already tagged. As nasty as the weather is today, people are going to be looking for jackets. Plus winter doesn't last forever. We only have a few months to sell these things."

"I agree," Laurie said. "And look here. I found more gloves and hats. We need to get these out pronto."

They spent half an hour squeezing as much warm clothing as possible onto the clothes racks. Their efforts were rewarded when a woman came in looking for a jacket and some sweatshirts. "Do you have any that will fit him?" She pointed to her son, a tall boy who looked distinctly uncomfortable to be the focus of attention.

"We just put a bunch of things out. I'll show you." Mary headed around the counter to lead the way.

"I'm not sure if you'll need to look at the boys' clothes or the men's."

"It just has to be warm. We're going up north for Christmas this year, and my aunt said it's been really cold."

Laurie was back at work tagging jewelry when a tall woman entered the shop and came into the office. "Hi, Evelyn. What's in the box?"

"Some old Christmas things. I bought new decorations at Dillard's. I just don't have room for these anymore." Evelyn set the box on the table and shrugged off her shearling coat to reveal a cashmere sweater and long tasseled necklace. "You can help me price these."

Evelyn had a way of ordering people around which usually annoyed Laurie, and today was no exception. *Lord give me strength. I work here for the customers*, she reminded herself, trying to keep her cool. She started sorting through the ornaments.

"Say, how's your little dog doing?" Laurie asked suddenly. "Is she all recovered from where the hawk or whatever it was attacked her?"

"Duchess is fully recovered," Evelyn said, a smile crossing her face. "Her fur is just about all grown back in. You can't even tell where that creature snatched her unless you know where to look, and you can't see the scar on her leg either, because of the fur. But you know, she stays right close to the fence almost underneath the shrubbery when I let her out to do her business, and she comes right back to the door when she's done. She's afraid something's going to swoop down and carry her away."

"Death comes from above. Dun-dun-dun," Mary said, sounding like an old movie trailer.

"But she still enjoys her walkies."

"You love your dog, don't you," Laurie said. *Probably your only virtue*, she thought. She held up a pair of ornaments. "What do you think on these? A quarter a piece?"

"Oh, no!" Evelyn said. "Those should be at least a dollar. Maybe a dollar and a half."

Laurie sighed, and grabbed a sheet of pricing dots and a pen. She knew disagreeing with Evelyn was pointless. The ornaments would probably sit in the shop until the last minute and then go for half price anyway. She wondered what it must have been like to grow up in Evelyn's world where everyone got a new set of Christmas ornaments each year.

Mary helped with the tagging, while Evelyn carried two handfuls of ornaments to the Christmas room. She came back shaking her head. "I don't know who bunched up the snowmen back there. Everything's a mess! If you've got those priced, I'll go straighten it out." She gathered the ornaments back into the box and carried them off.

"Gee, I don't know who bunched up the snowmen," Laurie said rolling her eyes. She pulled her phone out of her pocket and showed Mary the pictures she'd taken earlier.

Mary laughed. "Oh my God, it looks *awful*," she said in mock horror. Then she shrugged. "Whatever. It gives Evelyn something to do, besides ordering us around."

"I don't know where she gets off acting so superior all the time. I hope she leaves before she takes a good look at the clothes. She's liable to snatch all the winter things we just brought out and hang them in the back again."

"She likes to see daylight between each item. I don't get it," Mary said. "Customers aren't going to buy things they don't want just because that's all we have out for sale. The more we put out, the better the chance we'll sell something."

"That's the way I see it."

"I overheard her saying something to Carol at the church the other day." Mary leaned closer and lowered her voice. "She was griping because Virginia had given a couple of toys to those kids who come in with their grandpa all the time. You remember the guy who has diabetes so bad and his legs are so swollen?"

Laurie nodded. "I remember."

"Anyway, Evelyn was saying to Carol that we didn't need Virginia and she shouldn't be working here because she isn't a member of the church."

"As if we have so many volunteers!" Laurie said. "Cripe, we need as many warm bodies as we can get."

"That's what I think. But you know, Evelyn has had it out for Virginia for a long time, and she found out Virginia has a key now."

Laurie interrupted. "So Carol gave her a key too?"

"Same time as you got yours." Mary nodded. "It just makes sense. Hey, I would trust Virginia with the key to my house, let alone the key to the shop, but Evelyn..."

Mary broke off as the customer and her son came back to the counter. They purchased three sweatshirts, two jackets, and a pair of gloves, all of which Mary had just put out for sale. Laurie and Mary high-fived after the customers left the store.

Laurie turned the conversation back to Evelyn. "Seriously, she must have been some kind of spoiled," she said, looking around to be sure Evelyn couldn't overhear. "Was she an only child?"

"I think she has two brothers. Probably was spoiled though, the only girl in the family. But she does keep the place looking nice."

"Yep. They can put 'neat freak' on her tombstone. That's all she has going for her. Besides 'dog lover.'"

Mary shrugged. Both women had seen Evelyn in action. She might be bossy, but she wasn't afraid to tackle a hard or dirty job. And she did have an eye for display. She put in more than her share of time at the shop, as well as in the church helping out with the altar guild.

Evelyn reappeared in the office and dove for her coat. "Oh my gosh, is it that late? We have to go see Santa Claus this afternoon at the welcome center." The Chinkapin Welcome Center held a tree decorating contest as a fundraising event for a Christmas toy charity. The show was opening to the public with a surprise visit from St. Nick.

"Let us know how our tree looks," Mary said.

"I will. See you tomorrow." A gust of wind whipped Evelyn's coat around her as she dashed to her SUV.

"I already saw it," Laurie said in a sing-song voice.

"But the show doesn't open until today," Mary said.

"The judging was yesterday. Scott and I covered it for the paper." Scott was the editor for the newspaper where Laurie worked part time. "Guess you haven't seen today's *Journal* yet. And I was the one who convinced the St. Mark's flower guild to enter the contest. You know, public relations, and all that. They did a nice job, but the tree from the fire station won first prize. It was really cute."

"I would have thought the Chinkapin Arts Center would win," Mary said.

"They couldn't win. They did the judging."

"I'm glad St. Mark's at least had a tree in the show, so people will know we're here," Mary said.

"Right, so we don't have to keep calling it 'St. Mark's Across from the Tasty Chick.'" They both smiled at the church's long-time nick name. The Tasty Chick restaurant across the street was famous for their chicken tenders. It was also a great landmark for directing people to the church, and to the Treasure Chest next door.

"Speaking of Santa Claus," Laurie said, "I finally came up with the perfect idea for a Christmas present for Chase. You know, he kept saying he couldn't think of anything he wanted."

"So what was your great idea?"

"I've ordered a custom pet portrait of Beebee, the little dog Chase had growing up. A little pricey, but I think it'll be worth it." Laurie smiled smugly.

"Oh, that does sound nice. And it'll be something you can put in your new house." Mary got that mischievous look. "Will your friend Jeff be painting it?"

"Ha-ha." Laurie wrinkled her nose. "I make it a point to have as little to do with 'friend Jeff' as possible. No, I talked to Sharon yesterday at the arts center, and loaned her the photo of Beebee for reference." Laurie thanked heaven and all the guardian angels for keeping her from getting romantically involved with Jeff earlier in the year. He had turned out to be not as nice on the inside as he looked on the outside. And he sure did look nice on the outside, especially those striking blue eyes.

"I guess after seeing all the Christmas trees you must be in a festive mood," Mary said.

"Eh...not so much. It's too green outside. Back home it would be more wintry by now. I miss the fresh cold air, the brisk winter chill, the clear, starry nights." She closed her eyes, imagining the scene. It was Laurie's first winter in Georgia, and she wasn't used to the difference in climate. "It's too muggy here. I wish it would go ahead and rain. Plus, it's not really time for all these decorations. I can't believe how many people have their Christmas trees up already."

"Yeah, it's kind of a thing here to put them up the day after Thanksgiving. Some of our church friends wish we could decorate St. Mark's too. Mother Barbara has to keep reminding everyone it's advent."

"I just think it's wrong," Laurie said, folding her arms. Then she narrowed her eyes. "You haven't put your tree up yet, have you?" she asked Mary.

Her friend shrugged and smiled. "Well, when in Rome..."

Laurie rolled her eyes.

"You'll learn to like it. The nice thing about living in the south is that people can put up outdoor lights without freezing their tushes off, so I think it's prettier here."

"I might never decorate, in protest. Plus, what with buying the new house and saving up for furniture, we're sort of skipping Christmas, or at least keeping it low-key."

Laurie wouldn't admit it, but she felt downhearted about that. Mary must have noticed, because she changed the subject. "Now tell me again. What type of engagement ring are you looking for?"

"Something with some character. With a history behind it. I'll know it when I see it." Behind her back Laurie crossed her fingers.

Chapter 3.

Laurie left the Treasure Chest in a sprinkling rain and went straight to Chase's apartment. She found him at his kitchen table going over spreadsheets from his office at Anderson HVAC. She put her arms around his shoulders and kissed him on top of the head. "Are all the numbers adding up?" she asked.

"I'm not adding, I'm analyzing inventory so we can order supplies next week."

"Sounds fascinating," Laurie teased.

Chase grabbed her around the waist and gave her a playful squeeze. "Sugar, you need to work on your enthusiasm. 'Supplies used' correspond to 'jobs completed,' which adds up to me taking home a paycheck." He turned her loose and stuffed the spreadsheets into a folder. "But even I get tired of these numbers after a while."

He stood and gave her a proper hug and a kiss, and then looked into her eyes. "Still want to marry me?" he asked.

"Do I ever!" She kissed him back. "How's that for enthusiasm?"

"Maybe we don't want to go to the pawn shop." Chase ran his hand over her backside.

"Oh yes we do!" Laurie pulled away with a smile. "Now get your jacket. It's cold out there."

They dashed across the apartment's parking lot and into the pawn shop next door. "You know, this is the first time I've been in here." Laurie looked around curiously. "It's kind of like the Treasure Chest. It has a little bit of everything, and I don't know what half of the stuff is."

There were rows of power tools, musical instruments, and miscellaneous electronic items. Chase made a beeline for the instruments, and pulled a guitar down from where it hung suspended on a hook. He strummed twice, and then started tuning.

"Um, did you forget what we came here for?" Laurie asked.

"Hmm?" He continued tuning, sounding each string. Laurie glared at him. "Oops." Chase rehung the guitar and pointed. "The jewelry is up this way."

"How do you know where everything is?"

"I've been in here before. How do you think I keep the sound system at the church running? I've replaced most of the components with things I've bought here." He grew silent for a moment. "Plus I sold a ring here once." He had an earnest look on his face. "Full disclosure, remember? We agreed. I don't want us to have any more misunderstandings." He made air quotes at the word "misunderstandings." "I pawned my old wedding band here not long after I moved to Chinkapin."

Laurie nodded, her lips forming a silent "O," and squeezed his hand. When Laurie first started working at the Treasure Chest, a gold ring went missing from the jewelry case. Mother Barbara told her Chase had donated the ring to the thrift shop, but then needed money, and took the ring back without telling anyone. Laurie and Chase had both been through some rough times.

They climbed three steps at the back of the store and entered the jewelry section. Lighted display cases formed a horseshoe around three sides of the room. Chase nodded to a tall man standing behind the counter, who said, "Let me know if I can show you anything."

Laurie scanned the array of watches, bracelets, cigarette cases, compacts, and shiny objects of all sorts. Finally she came to a case full of rings: large men's rings with skulls or lion's heads on them; Masonic rings; mothers' rings; and finally engagement and wedding rings. "Look how they sparkle." Casually she asked Chase, "So, do you suppose your old ring is still here?"

Chase looked at her and then scanned the men's wedding bands. "It ... might have been that one." He pointed to a plain, yellow-gold band. "It was supposed to be comfortable. See how smooth and rounded it looks."

"Was it?"

"When we were happy it was," he said. "Later I couldn't wait to get it off." There was a hollow sound to his voice.

Laurie was sorry she had asked. She wanted them to enjoy the afternoon. Dredging up the past wasn't the way to do it. She took his hand and pulled him toward the other end of the display case. "Well, let's look at the ladies' rings first. I'm hoping to find something really wonderful."

He squeezed her hand and studied the rings in the case. "There sure are a lot to choose from," he said. "I know diamonds are a girl's best friend and all. Do you want it to shout *engagement ring*? Or do you want something different? One with a colored stone, maybe?"

"Something sparkly. Something pretty and romantic. Not the typical engagement ring, though.

And I don't want the interlocking kind. Those are okay, but if you wear the wedding band without the engagement ring, it looks a little weird."

"Why would you want to take them off?" Chase asked.

Laurie guessed he was thinking of his late wife Jenny's marital escapades. She hurried to reassure him. "Mary had to put away her diamond engagement ring because she scratched the baby with it a couple of times. Now she's not wearing much at all in the way of jewelry, other than her wedding band, since he broke one of her favorite necklaces. He's so grabby lately." She pointed to a gold band with a large central diamond and three smaller ones on either side. "Wow. That's pretty."

The clerk unlocked the case and lifted the ring out of the velvet tray. Laurie looked at the price tag and gasped. "Oh, I don't think so!"

"Try it on, just to see," Chase said.

She frowned at him. "It's eleven hundred dollars. No way am I interested in spending that. I might want to buy some furniture one of these days." She slipped it on her finger anyway. "Nah. It's a bit much," she said shaking her head and handing it back.

She looked at another one with art deco detailing on the band, and one stone. "What about that one?"

"A beautiful ring," the clerk said, slipping it from its place and handing it to her.

Laurie put it on her finger and admired it. "Do you like it?" she asked Chase.

"It's pretty. Not too plain, and it's sparkly."

"That ring will run you $2000. That's a very good diamond, and over six and a half carats."

"Oh," Laurie moaned, and quickly slipped it off again. "Okay. Show me something less expensive." She named a price range to the clerk, and whispered to Chase, "Why did I think they'd be less expensive at a pawn shop?"

The clerk replaced the ring, moved along to another section of the display case, and lifted out a velvet tray holding a dozen rings. "Do any of these interest you?"

Laurie's hand went immediately to a ring near the center of the tray. It had a single round diamond set in a circlet of white gold. The rest of the ring was yellow gold, with flowers and leaves carved halfway down the band on either side of the diamond.

"This is different. Isn't it pretty?" She slipped it on her finger, and turned her hand from side to side to watch the diamond sparkle. "Chase, I like this one.

It's simple, but it's not plain. I think it's romantic-looking, with the little flowers."

Chase nodded, and looked at the tray again. He pointed out a few others, but Laurie shook her head, and held onto the floral ring.

The clerk brought out another tray, and indicated several he thought Laurie might like. She tried on a white gold ring with three small diamonds, but quickly replaced it, and put on the floral ring again. "Tell me about this one I'm wearing. I'm afraid to look at the price tag."

"I think you'll be pleasantly surprised. That's a 1940's floral two-tone solitaire. One half carat."

"Wow! 1940's," Laurie said. She slipped it off and looked at the price tag. "But – why is this one so ..." She started to say cheap, but instead said, "inexpensive?"

The clerk brought out a little magnifier and handed it to Laurie. "Look closely at the diamond, and you'll be able to see that it's slightly imperfect."

She placed the magnifier to her eye and looked at the ring. "Is there something inside there?"

"That's an inclusion, a small imperfection in the diamond. All diamonds are unique because of the way they are formed. I doubt I've ever seen a diamond without some sort of flaw. The difference is in how large the inclusions are, where they are located, and so on. They do affect the clarity of the diamond, and in the wrong part of the stone they can affect its durability. This is a small feather inclusion deep within the diamond. Since you are more interested in the overall charm and appearance of the ring, I don't think it's a cause for concern. I just want you to understand why it's in this price range. It's a good quality ring, in excellent condition for its age, with a slightly imperfect stone."

"Hmmm," Laurie turned her hand from side to side, and took another look at the ring through the magnifier. Then she smiled at Chase. "We don't mind 'slightly imperfect,' do we?"

"I think it looks nice," Chase said. "If you wanted a ... whatever, a *clearer* stone, you couldn't get one this big and sparkly in this price range. Could you find a wedding band that would go with this, though?"

Laurie looked questioningly at the clerk.

"I have some paisley floral bands that might complement that engagement ring." He pulled out a tray of women's rings. "And here are similar men's rings, assuming you wanted them to match. This is a comfort band." He held one up for Chase to try. It was too large, and slid along his finger.

"What do you think?" he asked Laurie.

"I think it's pretty. It goes with this engagement ring." She still hadn't taken it off.

"Try some of the wedding bands," Chase said.

Laurie finally slipped the diamond ring off her finger and tried several of the bands. Her favorite was a small one with a smooth edge and floral detailing. She slid it on, and then placed the engagement ring behind it. "Look how nicely these go together." She laid her hand next to his, and suddenly found herself choking back a sob. Tears filled her eyes and spilled down her cheeks.

She buried her face in Chase's shoulder as he pulled her into his arms. They didn't separate until she stopped shaking. He brushed her hair aside gently and looked into her eyes. "Does that mean you like them," he murmured.

She nodded, and wiped her cheeks.

"We'll take these three," Chase said.

The clerk brought out a set of measuring rings. "Yours we'll have to resize, but I believe the lady's were fine as is?" He glanced at Laurie.

"They were. It was like they were made for me."

He slipped a measuring ring on Laurie's finger. "You happen to have a very popular ring size." He smiled. "So when is the big day?"

Chase and Laurie stared at each other, and then burst out laughing. "We don't know," Laurie said finally. "We're just so excited about being engaged! I guess we want to enjoy it for a while. What do you think, Chase?"

"I hadn't thought of a date. Sometime in the spring, or maybe earlier. Once winter's over, and before it gets too hot, anyway."

"Well, whenever it takes place, you'll have the rings. That will be one less thing to worry about."

As the clerk wrote up sizing instructions for the jeweler, Laurie walked around the room looking into the jewelry cases. "Look at these, Chase. Aren't they interesting?" Chase glanced over her shoulder at a display of antique keys. "Some of them are really ornate. And they're not very expensive. Look." They were displayed so that their price tags were visible. None was more than ten dollars, and others were only half that.

"Do you want one?" Chase asked.

"Oh," Laurie hesitated. "Not today. I think we've spent enough money. They are pretty, though." She turned away as the clerk handed paperwork to Chase and he paid for the rings.

Chapter 4.

"Shall we go somewhere to celebrate?" Chase pushed open the door of the pawn shop and stepped aside as Laurie joined him under the awning. Rain still pattered down from the leaden sky.

"Yes," Laurie nodded. "I need to warm up. It was cold in there, even with all the lights shining on the jewelry. I'm so excited about our rings!"

"Me too," Chase said, kissing her on the lips. "The Coffee Pot?"

"Just what I was thinking." She pulled her hood up and they walked quickly to Laurie's Malibu parked in the lot next door.

Laurie had been visiting the Coffee Pot on a regular basis since moving to Chinkapin. It was one of her favorite spots. The café was decorated in a 1930's and '40's theme, and Laurie loved all the vintage details down to the Formica-topped tables, the chrome-and-vinyl chairs, and the tiles on the floor. She especially loved the music floating from the sound system, punctuated by the steamy gurgle of the espresso machine.

The smell of freshly ground coffee welcomed them inside. Laurie glanced in the pastry case and then looked up at the menu board.

"You getting your usual?" Chase asked.

"No. I think I'll have... Give me a large salted caramel latte. That sounds good. And a piece of the crumb cake." She smiled at Chase. "I'm celebrating."

"I reckon all that shopping took a lot out of you," he said grinning.

"Hey, I did work at the Treasure Chest for four hours today." She put her hands on her hips and stretched up to her full five feet six inches.

"Peace! Just watch what I order." He requested a toffee nut latte and a brownie with walnuts. "See, all the nuts are good for me, and the chocolate has antioxidants. Plus, we might as well both be buzzed on caffeine."

While the barista made their drinks, they took their desserts to a table near the wall. Laurie sat next to Chase and pointedly stared at the bag from the jewelry store.

"I was thinking of giving the engagement ring to you on Christmas day," he said.

Laurie's jaw dropped, and she wrinkled her brow. She saw the corner of Chase's mouth twitch as he tried not to laugh. "Argh! You're so mean," she said. "Give me that ring." He handed over the bag, and Laurie pulled out the small velvet box. It made a creaking sound when she opened it. She smiled, admiring the ring as she turned the box from side to side.

"Ooh, is that for me?" The server brought their drinks to the table and leaned over to look in the box.

"Oh, no you don't." Laurie pulled it close, and the server laughed and walked back to the counter. Then Laurie held the box out to Chase. "Will you do the honors? You don't have to go down on one knee again."

"You're not going to cry, are you?"

"No. I did all the crying in the pawn shop. I just want my ring!"

"Maybe we should wait until we get home."

"Charles Wesley Harris, you give me that ring right now!"

He laughed, and pulled the ring from its groove in the ring box. Laurie's stomach fluttered as he held it up and said, "Laura May, will you marry me?"

She laughed. "How could I resist those puppy-dog eyes?" Chase slipped the ring into place. "I feel sugar-high and I haven't even eaten my cake." She admired her hand, and then lifted her cup. "A toast: to a long and happy marriage."

He lifted his mug and clinked it against hers. "Long and happy."

Laurie closed her eyes and took a sip.

"Looks like you two are celebrating," a familiar voice said nearby.

Laurie opened her eyes. "Hi, Chad. How are you?" She held her left hand casually up to her cheek. That and her bright smile were all the clues the realtor needed.

"Well, I'll be. Look at the sparkle on that diamond. Ooh, Lord, it's a beauty for sure." Chad Houser worked for Chinkapin Realty. He didn't know it, but Chase had proposed to Laurie just moments after Chad showed them through the house that they had decided to purchase. The realtor patted Chase on the back. "You done good there, buddy."

"Laurie's cheeks will be hurting tonight, she's been smiling so much," Chase said, looking like he might feel the same. "Hey, I'm glad you stopped in here. We were going to call you next week. How soon do you think we can get what's-his-name, Frank, to get in the house and do the home inspection?"

"Well, sorry to say, everything's at a standstill right now. Frank just had an emergency appendectomy."

"What?! When did this happen?"

"Yesterday morning. He told me he wasn't feeling right. He found out why, and just in the nick of time. His appendix was fixing to burst."

"And there's no one else who can do the inspection?"

"I've called half a dozen people, and haven't found anyone yet. But I'll keep looking! Don't abandon hope."

"It's getting awfully close to Christmas though," Laurie said, shoulders slumping. "I have a feeling we won't be closing any time soon."

"Sorry." The realtor shook his head. "But it probably won't happen until well into the new year."

"Well, we've been in our apartments this long. What's another month? Besides," Laurie added, "we don't have any furniture. Even if we could move in to the house, we'd be sleeping on the floor."

"I was hoping to get in and do some painting while business is slow, though" Chase said. "Now what?"

"Well, I can check with the sellers. The Hinsdales may not care if you get in early." Chad scratched his jaw and looked at Chase. "To tell the truth, you probably know as much about home inspection as Frank does. You can look the house over yourself next week sometime. I'll go with you, if you want another pair of eyes. Then if you're satisfied, we'll go ahead with the paperwork, and you can still get in early to get the painting started."

"That's a good idea, isn't it?" Laurie's face brightened.

Chase nodded. "I'd like to poke around, get a closer look at the plumbing and things."

"Want to set it for Monday, then?" Chad asked.

"I have to go into work in the morning, see what jobs we have lined up and order some materials. How about Monday afternoon?" Chase said.

"Sounds like a plan, buddy. I'll call you Monday morning to firm up the time. I don't want to interrupt your little celebration here. Congratulations again!" Chad and Chase shook hands, and the realtor walked back to the counter to place his order.

"If you go to inspect the house Monday afternoon, I can meet you there and kind of look around," Laurie said. "It feels strange to not have any furniture to speak of. Even the first time I got married I had hand-me-down furniture, and stuff I'd bought during my last year in college. Now I've just got a desk, and my childhood bedroom stuff in storage at Mary's house."

"Isn't this better, though?" Chase asked. "This way it'll be *our* furniture, and not things left over from our previous lives."

"I guess it's better. Just ... strange."

* * *

Chase cooked supper that evening while Laurie went up to her own apartment to work on her manicure. She wanted her hands to look perfect when she got to church the next morning and showed everyone her ring. She always kept her nails fairly short anyway, because it made it easier to type. She didn't know how women did it with the long, fancy nails. She smoothed her nails with a four-way buffer and added a coat of clear polish.

She slipped her engagement ring off just long enough to slather on a good layer of hand cream. Then she put the ring back on and admired her hands. "I love it," she said aloud. At least the rings were taken care of.

Funny that they hadn't set a date yet. She hadn't thought about it until the guy at the pawn shop asked when the wedding was. Sometime in the spring, Chase had said. She hoped it would be even sooner, but for now that would do.

The location was already in the bag. No question but that the wedding would be at St. Mark's. After all, that was where she and Chase had met, up in the choir loft. She would have to make sure Steve was available to play the organ.

She only had a vague notion about the service itself. She planned to take notes during Luke and Cory's wedding in Peach Valley the following weekend. Come to think of it, the service was in the prayer book. She would just look it over in church the next morning.

And as for her reception, Laurie figured it would be at St. Mark's also. She wished there were a way to make the parish hall a little less drab, but there was only so much you could do with cinder-block walls and aluminum windows.

She did a little mental calculation about how many people might attend. Her family and Chase's, for sure; some of their friends from church; maybe a couple of co-workers of hers from the *Journal*, and Chase's from the HVAC company. It could be a pretty large crowd, the more she thought about it. What would finger food and cake cost for that many people?

The thought of food made Laurie hungry, so she went down the stairs to Chase's apartment. She could hear his music playing from out in the hall.

"I've just been thinking about our wedding," she announced as she came in.

Chase put a couple of forks on the table and grabbed Laurie in his arms. "For you, for me, forever more," he crooned, pulling her into a foxtrot. "This is great music. Did you know the Gershwin's wrote this? I think Artie Shaw's version was the most popular."

Their dance was interrupted by the kitchen timer. Chase released her and put on a set of oven mitts.

"I said, I've been thinking about our wedding," Laurie repeated, placing plates on the table.

"Not getting cold feet, are you?" he asked.

"Oh, no. Just thinking about the service, and the reception, and all. There could be a pretty good crowd there."

"Yeah?" Chase wrinkled his brow as he placed a pan of lasagna on the table. "What do you mean by 'pretty good'?"

"Oh, seventy-five or so. When you add up our parents and siblings, their spouses, people from work, from church, and maybe a few from around town that we've gotten to be friends with. That's a lot of cake and finger foods."

"We could just elope," Chase said. "Go somewhere in the mountains. Gatlinburg maybe. Or to South Carolina. Or we could go to the coast and have a beach wedding."

"Eh," Laurie said wrinkling her nose. "Too much sand everywhere. But you know, I already did the big, fancy wedding goat rope. I'm not sure I need to do it again."

"I did too, but not with you," Chase said.

That made Laurie pause. She took a bite of lasagna. "Mmm. This is good. We could feed them all lasagna."

"That's an idea," Chase said.

"I'll be interested to see what Luke and Cory do at their wedding next week." She put it out of her mind, and concentrated on Chase's excellent lasagna.

* * *

Sunday morning Laurie slipped on a rose-red sweater, black slacks, and added a small silver necklace and earrings. She brushed out her hair, slipped on her flats, and smiled at her refection. "Hi," she said to the mirror, waving her left hand. The diamond sparkled in the light over the bathroom mirror.

Her stomach fluttered a little as she and Chase made the short drive to St. Mark's. They parked in the Treasure Chest lot as usual, walked across to the church, and hung their jackets on the long rack in the hallway. Then they made their way up to the choir loft.

Laurie waved to her choir friends, and was disappointed when no one noticed her new ring. She took her seat and glanced at the bulletin waiting for Mary to arrive.

"Oh, Lord, that little man is going to be the death of me," Mary said as she plopped into a seat next to Laurie. "I had Ricky dressed up all cute and then he threw up all over himself, me, the changing table ..." She sighed and picked up her hymnal, glanced at the bulletin and starting marking pages with ribbons.

Laurie hadn't said anything, so finally Mary looked at her. "So how are you this morning? Did you guys do anything fun yesterday?" Suddenly she remembered. She grabbed Laurie's left hand and pulled it toward her eyes with a gasp. "Well, that's pretty! I've never seen anything like it. Look at the little flowers around the sides, and that diamond! Oh, your man did good!"

Suddenly Mary stood up. "Everybody, I have an announcement to make." She raised Laurie's hand in the air like a prize fighter. "I think you all know that Laurie and Chase are engaged." She looked around for Chase in the row behind them, who sat with his arms folded, happily watching the proceedings. "Well, it's official. Behold the ring!"

Laurie hadn't blushed in a while, but with all the attention she could feel her cheeks glowing. Suddenly the organ erupted with the strains of the bridal chorus from Wagner's "Lohengrin." After a few bars Steve cut it short. "We interrupt this engagement party for a choir rehearsal. Can I get you all to do some warm-ups, please?"

The rest of the choir warmed up, but Mary and Laurie whispered together as Mary examined the ring. "So where did this come from? Tell me all about it."

"Chinkapin pawn shop. Isn't it different? It's from the 1940's. I love it. We picked wedding bands too. The bands match, and they look really pretty next to my engagement ring."

"Very nice." Mary looked at Laurie, and then put her arm around her in a side hug. "I'm happy for you," she whispered. She turned and flashed a thumbs-up at Chase, who smiled and nodded.

The service finally got underway, with the normal procession through the nave and back into the choir loft, the prayers, hymns, and readings. Finally Mother Barbara proclaimed, "The peace of the Lord be always with you."

"And also with you," rumbled through the nave and the choir loft, and parishioners turned to their neighbors offering hugs and handshakes. The passing of the peace was always a leisurely affair at St. Mark's, as people greeted those seated around them, or moved through the nave to welcome newcomers. Finally everyone returned to their seats for the announcements.

"I'd like to call your attention to the information on the back of the bulletin," Mother Barbara said. There was a request for volunteers to assist with a couple of clean-up days; one to be held inside the church during the week, and the other to spruce up the church grounds the following Saturday.

"Are you and Chase going to make it?" Mary asked Laurie.

Laurie shook her head. "I don't know. We're going to that wedding in Peach Valley. You know, Luke, who runs the bookstore there, and Cory from the university?"

Mary nodded, and held her hand up to shush Laurie while Mother Barbara announced the date for the greening of the church. "You *have* to come to that. It's in the afternoon on the last Sunday before Christmas. First we decorate the church, and then there's a party in the parish hall afterwards."

"Sounds like fun. I'm sure we're free then." Laurie turned in her seat and caught Chase's eye. She pointed to the announcement about the greening of the church in the bulletin.

"Count me in," he said.

Chapter 5.

Monday morning Laurie had one eye on the items she was editing for the *Journal's* events column, and her other eye on her cell phone as she waited for a text from Chase. Work was slow. A lot of the Christmas events had been submitted weeks ago, and few new items were coming in this late in the season.

Laurie checked the City of Chinkapin Facebook page, and noted a couple of upcoming events she wanted to cover for the paper. She was just reading about a benefit performance at the little theater when her phone finally dinged. She was surprised to see a text from Sharon at the Chinkapin Arts Center.

Bad news – call me

Laurie quickly found Sharon's number and placed the call. "Hi, Sharon. What's up? I hope the news isn't *too* bad."

"You're not going to be happy, but it's nothing I can control. I have to go to South Carolina. My grandmother broke her hip and just got out of the hospital. Mom was supposed to take care of her, but now she's down with bronchitis, and is afraid if she goes up there she'll pass it on to Grandma. I'm the only other person Mom can call on to take over, so I'm going up tomorrow morning."

"Uh-oh."

"I guess you figured out that I won't be able to do the painting of Beebee you wanted. Unless you can wait for it for a couple of months."

Laurie groaned. "A couple of *months?*" Chase still hadn't provided any hints about what he wanted for Christmas, and Laurie was counting on the portrait of his childhood chiweenie to be a nice surprise. "That won't work. I mean, I'm sorry about your grandmother, but ..."

"Now, the other thing you could do is let Jeff do the painting. I asked him this morning, when he was here teaching his class, and he said he could paint it for you, if you want him to."

Laurie had to think about that. Jeff Williams was the last person she wanted to work with. She felt awkward about having made out with him once (before she had started going with Chase). She also thought there must be some ill feelings on Jeff's part, since she had cost him a lot of money. Thousands of dollars, in fact.

The Treasure Chest had donated an old painting to the Chinkapin Arts Center which Jeff realized was a valuable watercolor by Winslow Homer. When he sold it with the intention of keeping all the profits, he ensured his spot as one of Laurie's least favorite people of all time. He only split the money with the thrift shop and the arts center when she threatened to ruin his reputation by exposing his greed.

"Jeff, huh?" she said, still unsure.

"You know he's actually better at pet portraits than I am," Sharon said. Laurie knew it was true. Sharon's forte was landscapes and florals. "He'd do a good job for you."

Laurie made up her mind. "You know, yeah, I think that's what I want to do. Do I need to call him, or something?"

"No," Sharon said. "I'll stop in his gallery this afternoon. I'll drop off the photo of Beebee that you gave me, and give him the go-ahead, tell him what we discussed, the cost we agreed on, and everything."

Laurie was relieved not to have to deal with Jeff any more than necessary. "Please, just don't let anything happen to that photo. It's the only picture of Beebee that Chase has."

"Not to worry. Thanks for understanding, and I'll tell Jeff to be in touch with you if he has any questions."

"Okay. Talk to you later. Safe travels, and I hope your grandma gets better soon." Laurie hung up, a little unhappy about this turn of events.

She was still staring at her phone when she finally got the text from Chase.

Heading to the house now. Meet you there. Bring coffee

Laurie sent him back a hearts emoji, switched off everything at her desk, and drove to the Coffee Pot.

She ordered two lattes, plus a bagel and cream cheese for herself, since she was starving, and drove around the block to 501 Evergreen Drive. Chase's truck and the realtor's car stood in the driveway, so Laurie parked across the street.

She stood on the curb lawn for a moment admiring the house. Then she grabbed the coffees and her snack, and proceeded up the brick walkway toward the wood-frame two-story cottage. She loved the tall oak tree in the yard, and was grateful to the previous owners who, for whatever reason, had left the front porch swing and wicker furniture behind. It still surprised her to see green leaves on rosebushes in December. Stout branches clung to the trellis behind the swing at one end of the porch.

She was just wondering how she would manage opening the door with her hands full when Chase appeared.

"Ah, coffee, it's so good to see you. I mean Laurie! It's so good to see you."

"Aren't we in a merry mood," she said, holding the coffee out of reach.

He snatched a cup from her hand, took a grateful swig and smacked his lips. "I'm remembering all the things we liked about this place. Come on in." He held the door as she stepped into the foyer and turned to face the fireplace. "We haven't got much farther than the living room, but the bricks and the damper on the fireplace are all sound."

The realtor entered from the kitchen. "Hi, Chad," Laurie said. "I'm sorry I didn't think to ask if you wanted anything."

He waved away the thought. "I had my fill of doughnuts and coffee back at the office. Chase, I think you'll be happy with the water heater. It looks almost new. Apparently they installed one with a larger tank when they added the new kitchen and the extra bathroom."

Chase kissed Laurie on the cheek. "Back to work," he said, grabbing his flashlight from where it sat on the hearth.

"I'm going to poke in the cupboards and closets, and figure out where we can put things." Laurie went into the large kitchen and munched her bagel while she opened cupboards and drawers and looked in the pantry.

Between her and Chase they might be able to outfit a kitchen, but neither of them owned a decent set of china or glassware. Chase loved to cook, and had assembled a fair amount of cookware and enough dishes for two people to eat from. Laurie had fewer things in her apartment, but what she did have were beautiful or interesting pieces she had picked up at the Treasure Chest. She figured wedding gifts would help to fill in the gaps, if she and Chase could just set a date. And send out invitations.

She wiped her lips on her napkin, took one more sip of her latte, and headed upstairs.

The old house had originally had three bedrooms and a bathroom upstairs, but with the addition of the new kitchen, den, and powder room on the main floor they'd added a room above, along with a second full bath. The new room had a lot of windows, most of which faced the back yard. The realtor had called it a bonus room, but Laurie thought it could be a nice master bedroom. The only problems was it had just one closet, and not a huge one at that. Where would all her clothes fit?

She looked at the other bedrooms. Two were of almost equal size. One would serve as a guest room. Laurie had hazy ideas that the other would be a child's room, one day.

The smallest of the bedrooms was only half the size of the others, though it had two windows. It might make a lovely nursery, or an office, or even a dressing room.

Laurie looked curiously at the narrow closet in the little room. Instead of extending all the way to the floor, the door stopped about eight inches above the baseboard, making it more of a tall built-in cupboard. She walked out of the room and looked around the corner. There was the staircase, right under the little room, and the closet, or cupboard, extended out over the stairway.

The walls inside the cupboard were all made of the same wood as the floors, and the back of the closet slanted backwards over the stairs, deeper at the top than at the bottom.

Laurie knew it wouldn't hold much in the way of clothes, though it might be fitted with shelves. With a hand on one hip, she looked around the room considering her options. She already owned a hope chest and a chest of drawers from her old bedroom set. What if she added a vanity? Or a wardrobe, a cheval mirror, and a lovely slipper chair? She could make it into a chic boudoir. She pictured a little chandelier hanging from the ceiling.

Chase called her from the main floor. "I'm up here," she answered. "Come tell me what you think about my idea."

On a whim, she stepped up into the cupboard and pulled the door nearly shut. As Chase ascended the stairs just beneath her, she held her breath and leaned back against the wall.

"Laurie? Which room are you in?" His voice faded as he went the wrong way.

"The little one next to the stairs," she called through the crack in the door.

She peaked out as Chase entered and looked around, scratching his head. "Not much room for someone to hide in," he said, and pulled the closet door open.

Laurie held her hands crossed over her chest. "Good evening," she said in her best Bela Lugosi voice.

"You nut," Chase said. "This is weird." He looked past her at the back of the closet. "I guess they didn't want to waste any space. Still, it doesn't seem very useful, the way the back wall tilts backwards."

"No, but it could be a linen cupboard, if you added some shelves."

She reached for Chase's shoulder and meant to step lightly down, but something caught her heel and she tumbled out on top of him. He caught her before she hit the floor. "Whoa, Nellybelle," he said. "You need to get your feet under you first."

"My shoe was stuck on something," Laurie said. She ran her hand along the bottom of the closet, and quickly pulled it away. "There's a hole in the back, like a knot hole." She ran her hand along it again. "A big knot hole." She stuck all four fingers into the hole, and was surprised when a section of board lifted up. "Look!" She removed the board and handed it to Chase.

He peered curiously into the closet. "Maybe it's an old access panel, though why that would be over the stairs ... All the plumbing is across the hall, so that's not it."

"Can you see wiring, or anything? Here, let's use your flashlight." Laurie pulled it out of his back pocket and switched it on.

She raised the light, shining it into the space, and gasped. "It's a secret compartment," she said. "And there's something in here."

Chapter 6.

Laurie fumbled with one hand in the compartment, finally giving the flashlight back to Chase. "Here, hold this." She reached in with both hands, and pulled out a wooden box.

"Wow," Chase said. "That's ... dusty." He trailed a finger along the top revealing dull mahogany under the dust. "Looks like it could use some lemon oil. Will it open?"

Laurie pulled up on the edges. "It's locked." She ran a finger over a tiny, brass-rimmed keyhole on the front.

"Is it a jewelry box? Or a silverware box?"

"Seems a little small for a silverware box," Laurie said. "It's shaped more like a ... like a tea caddy. Maybe a writing box. Or just a sewing box or a trinket box."

"Maybe there's a pair of pearl-handled pistols in there. Or someone's ashes," Chase suggested, raising his eyebrows. "Give it here."

Laurie handed him the box and he shook it up and down and from side to side a couple of times. "Sounds like there's something in it, but it's not very heavy, so it's not Spanish doubloons, or the lost gold of the confederacy. Maybe just letters. Or stock certificates!" He rubbed the dust off the top and wiped his hand on his pants.

"Ooh. Either of those could be interesting," Laurie said.

She jumped at a sound in the hall, and turned as Chad entered the room. "What's next, Chase?" he asked.

"Did you know this little closet had a secret compartment in it?" Laurie said. "Look here." She held up the panel and Chase shone his flashlight into the space in the closet.

Chad leaned over and looked inside where the section of flooring had been removed. "Well, dang. Ain't that something." He looked at the box. "And this box was in there?"

Laurie nodded. "Nice wood, isn't it? Although the box is really rather plain. Doesn't look like it could be very important, except that it's locked. You haven't come across any keys, have you?"

"Nope. Nothing like that."

Laurie took the flashlight and leaned over to shine it around in the compartment. "There's not room for much more in here. The compartment goes back over the stairs a few inches, and then stops. Not that I really want to stick my hand in and feel around back there."

"I'll do it," Chase said. "Hold the box."

Laurie handed him the flashlight. She took the box, held it up closer to her ear and shook it from side to side as Chase felt around in the closet.

"Nope. Nada," he said.

"I guess I'll take a few pictures, and notify the Hinsdales that you found it here," Chad said. "By rights it's theirs, at least until you buy the place."

"It's not 'finders keepers'?" Chase asked.

"No," Laurie said. "We shouldn't keep something that doesn't really belong to us." She thought of Jeff, her artist "friend."

Laurie held up the box and Chad snapped a couple of pictures. Then he texted them to the owners of the house, who were now living in a downtown Chicago condominium.

"I guess I'll put it back, for now?" Laurie said uncertainly.

"Might as well," Chase agreed.

She set the box back in the compartment. Chase fitted the board into place, and pulled his head back out of the closet. "I don't know how you ever found the notch back there. I guess your fingers are smaller than mine."

"Even a blind squirrel finds a nut once in a while," Laurie said.

"You're a nut," he said, and kissed her.

"What else would you like to look at today?" Chad said, interrupting their romantic moment.

Chase and Laurie exchanged a look. "I think we've seen it all. When you hear from the owners, find out if it's all right for us to start painting. Meanwhile Laurie and I can look at colors and shop for furniture."

"I'll let you know as soon as I hear from them, and I'll also let you know what they say about that box. We might just be able to have the closing you wanted before New Year."

"Hey," Laurie said suddenly. "Send me those pictures you took of the box. I want to show a friend of mine."

"I surely will. And I'll make sure everything here is locked up," Chad said. The two men shook hands.

Second Home

"I gotta go back to work," Chase said as he and Laurie parted with a kiss on the front porch. "See you this evening."

"See you," she said. She got in her car, and pulled up Mary's number on her cell phone.

* * *

"Hey, friend," Laurie said over the car's Bluetooth as she paused at the corner of Main Street and Redding Road. "Do you still want to do some shopping with me?"

"Sure thing," Mary said eagerly. She and little Ricky were usually ready for a shopping trip.

"On my way." Laurie pulled off Redding Road and onto Mary's street. She remembered how envious she used to be of Mary's neighborhood. She still thought it was pretty posh, but it didn't have the charm and vintage character of Evergreen Drive. She parked on one side of the driveway, leaving room so Mary's car with the baby seat could pull out.

"As soon as we start driving he'll probably fall asleep," Mary said, answering the front door with the baby on her hip. "But, so be it. Come on in. I just need to tuck a few things into the diaper bag. Here, take Ricky."

"Oof," Laurie grunted, settling the baby in her arms. "What are you feeding this kid?" She followed her friend through the house toward the nursery, noting the playpen in the living room, the toys scattered on the floor, and the high chair which was now a permanent fixture in the kitchen. Laurie had pictured her new house with various configurations of furniture, draperies, and rugs, but hadn't got so far as picturing it with all the paraphernalia a baby would require. Where was that longing for a baby that had consumed her a few months back? Had it just been jealousy over her friend's newborn?

"I was just over at the house on Evergreen," she said. "Chase wanted to check it out himself, since the inspector was delayed again. And I wanted to look around and get some ideas about which room we'll use as the master, and which rooms we'll want to paint."

"You should have called me! I can't wait to see inside. Is everything looking good over there?" Mary asked, gathering baby items.

"Oh, yeah. But get this. I'm thinking of turning the littlest bedroom into a dressing room slash boudoir type of thing, and I was poking around in the closet, and guess what: I found a secret compartment."

"No way. Was there something in it?"

"A wooden box, and it was locked."

"What? Are you serious? How big of a box? What kind of a box?" Mary had stopped what she was doing and looked at Laurie wide-eyed. "I hope there are no body parts in it."

"Funny you should say that, because Chase thought maybe it could be someone's ashes. But it wasn't really big enough or heavy enough for much in the way of body parts."

"Maybe someone's heart. You know, like the wicked queen wanted the huntsman to cut out Snow White's heart and bring it back in a box? 'Bring me her heart,'" Mary said in a "wicked queen" voice.

"Mary, have you been reading murder mysteries again?"

"No," she said defensively. "Just paranormal romance. I can give you some recommendations." She lifted her eyebrows.

"Maybe after the honeymoon," Laurie said. "Anyway, here." She set the baby down on the changing table and pulled her phone out of her purse. "Here's the box."

Mary examined the pictures which the realtor had texted to Laurie. "Oh, yeah. Too small for many body parts. Maybe desiccated eyeballs?"

"Oh, my God, who are you?" Laurie laughed, putting away her phone and picking up the baby again. "It's not empty, anyway. I could hear something shifting from side to side when I shook it. Like paper or something. Probably just someone's old checkbook registers or tax papers, but it's fun to wonder."

"You didn't try to pry it open?" Mary continued asking questions as they walked out to the garage and she put Ricky into his car seat.

"Well, we don't own the house yet, so any contents not specified as being sold with the house belong to the owners in Chicago. Chad is getting in touch with them to see what they want to do with it."

"Well, maybe the key will turn up, and then you could at least peek inside."

Laurie wondered about the ethics of that for a minute. If the box had been unlocked, or she had just found the contents of the box lying loose in the little hiding place, she certainly would have had a look.

"Okay, where are we going again?" Mary asked as she finally backed the car out of her driveway.

"I wanted to try the other thrift shops in town before I settle on that dress at the Treasure Chest."

"Right. Well, let's go to Top Dog first, and see if they have anything." Mary's car knew the way to all the thrift shops within thirty miles of her house. It helped her stick to the deal she'd made with her husband Pete when they'd first moved to Chinkapin. If they could stay within their household budget on his salary, she didn't have to go back to work.

Some of the glamour had worn off being a public school music teacher, which Mary was by training, and she had wanted to start a family and stay home while her kids were young. Consequently, she did her best to stick to the budget.

Affordable Elegance, as Mary called it, and its companion, *Affordable Baby*, had turned into a fun challenge for her. Part of her strategy was thrift and consignment shopping. She gladly shared her strategy with others, and had a lively following on Instagram, where she originally started posting pictures of Ricky in his "thrift shop threads." With Laurie's help, Mary also had written a couple of articles for the *Journal* on shopping the local thrift shops, estate sales, and consignment shops, and the two now ran a regular column in the newspaper, "The Rummage Roundup," advertising all of the above.

"So you're looking for something elegant, affordable, and ... tell me again?" Mary asked.

"Luke and Cory's wedding is in the afternoon, so something I can wear for that, and also maybe for the Christmas party Chase is having for the HVAC employees and families. Sort of Christmas-y, but not 'ugly-sweater' Christmas-y. You know what I'm dreaming of? Something velvet, in like a jewel tone. Like an old-fashioned velvet dress with three-quarter sleeves, and a lace collar ..."

"Hmm. Maybe we should be looking in *antique* stores instead of thrift shops." Mary sounded disapproving.

"Well, what would you get?"

"A little black dress. String of pearls, if you want to get all traditional on me."

"Black dress for a wedding? And Christmas party?"

"Leave it to mother Mary to dress you in style," Mary said tossing her head.

Laurie looked at Mary's outfit, which today consisted of gray leggings, a long navy sweatshirt atop a turtleneck, and a pair of gray wool sneakers. "I hear you. 'Pay no attention to the man behind the curtain,'" she said.

"What's wrong with my outfit?"

"Nothing, nothing. I certainly know nothing about fashion, so far be it from me to criticize."

"Okay, be quick in here," Mary said as she parked outside the first shop. "I want to go to Georgia

Thriftique." She gently unloaded the sleeping baby from his car seat, and followed Laurie into the shop.

Top Dog was a fund-raising arm for the Chinkapin Animal Shelter, so many of the thrift shop's items were a bit on the wild side. Laurie looked around briefly at the pet-related items in the front of the shop, and then walked on into the larger room beyond.

Housewares, home décor, and sporting goods were loosely organized around the room, with a long clothing rack in the middle. Laurie browsed through the clothing, but quickly grew frustrated. Things were jammed together, and when Laurie tried to shove them to one side so she could examine individual items, a couple of them fell off their hangers and she had to take time to re-hang them.

"Hmph," Mary said from the other side of the rack. "I like the way the Treasure Chest does it better. At least we don't have a lot of summer items out in December." She moved along down the rack. "I'm not seeing many dresses at all. Oh! Here it is." She pulled a sweater out of the rack and held it up. It had an appliqued Christmas tree with lots of sequins, and small three-dimensional presents sewn on around the bottom." Ricky lifted his head from her shoulder, rubbed his eyes, and stared at the sweater, reaching for a little box under the tree.

"Lovely," Laurie said. "Look, I'll hunt for something for me, while you look at the baby items."

Mary laughed and wandered around the shop, naming things out loud for Ricky's benefit.

Laurie finally gave up on the clothing rack, and turned her attention to a display of necklaces and bracelets hung on a pegboard, with rings, earrings, and other small items in a tray below. A shiny object caught her eye.

"Look at this," Laurie said holding up a small brass key. It was plain, with an oval loop at the top, and two teeth at the bottom.

Mary came to stand next to her. "What about it?"

"Maybe it's the key to that box."

Mary shrugged. "Buy it and find out."

"I think I will. I'm ready to check out. Did you find anything?"

"These. What do you think?" Mary held up a pair of fuzzy brown slippers with teddy bear faces on the toes. Ricky reached for them, and she let the baby hold them.

"Cute."

They made their purchases, loaded the little one in the car seat, and proceeded to their next stop.

Georgia Thriftique looked more promising, or at least had a lot more clothes, arranged by garment type. Laurie headed straight for the dresses, with Mary behind her pushing Ricky in his stroller.

"If I were sixteen and on my way to the prom this place would be a gold mine," Laurie said. She examined the dresses one at a time and then slid them on down the rack. Most were sleeveless or off-the-shoulder, and a number of them were so short Laurie wondered whether they were dresses at all and not tunics.

"I know what you mean. I get a chill looking at these. Don't dressmakers know how to do sleeves anymore?"

"I'd have to wear my mink jacket to stay warm," Laurie said.

"You have a mink jacket?" Mary asked.

"No. I'm kidding!"

"Last year at the Treasure Chest we had one. It was beautiful, and so soft! It wasn't there long, though. Sharon from the arts center snapped it up. It looked great on her."

"How about that. I'm surprised Evelyn didn't take it to Redding, to that fur shop up there. I know they take pre-owned furs on consignment."

"That does sound like something Evelyn would do," Mary agreed. "She must have been on vacay when the fur was donated."

"Look. What do you think of this? What is this, like emerald? Or hunter green? Maybe I could shorten it?" Laurie held up a full-length deep green velvet dress, with long sleeves that puffed at the shoulder.

"I think Mrs. Claus donated that dress. It's not very sexy. I know you want something for winter, but," she shook her head. "It just doesn't have any pizzazz. And it would cost more than it's worth to have it altered. Check out this little number." She held up a champagne cocktail dress with crystal pleats and a deep V neck.

"Are you serious?" Laurie snorted. "Not my style."

"What about this?" Mary held up a black sheath.

Laurie stuck her tongue out. "Do you know how wide my butt would look in that thing? I need a little camo around my hips."

Suddenly Laurie stopped sliding hangers along the rack, and looked intently at a claret velvet dress. "Hmmm. I have a feeling this would look better with a body in it. What do you think?"

Mary frowned at the dress, her eyebrows scrunched together. "I like the color. Like you said, it's hard to tell, on the hanger. Try it on if you want. I'll come over to the fitting room in a minute."

Laurie walked across the shop to the fitting rooms along the wall. It took her a moment to remove her jacket and all her clothes, but finally she pulled the dress over her head, zipped it up the back, and turned to examine her reflection in the mirror.

The dress had three-quarter sleeves and a high mandarin collar, with a frog closure over a keyhole opening. The fitted bodice flattered her waist, which Laurie always thought of as one of her better features, and the loosely fitting skirt skimmed her hips and ended elegantly at mid-calf. Laurie loved the color of the dress against her skin. She held up her hair, imagining it in a loose chignon, and stood on tiptoes. A new pair of heels might be in order.

"Laurie. Are you in there?" Mary's voice called from outside. Laurie unbolted the door and swung it open, watching her friend's face.

"Ooh, I like that!" Mary nodded, wide eyed. "Twirl for me," she said drawing a circle with her finger.

Laurie twirled. The skirt whirled gently around her legs.

"That is *really* pretty. The color is nice, and the fitted bodice with the little keyhole makes it a little sexy, but not like you're selling something. It's kind of elegant. I think it's perfect. Just add a pair of black heels, and a little black evening bag. Hey, we have a pretty little bag in our shop."

"I'm glad you like it, because I already decided I'm done shopping. I'm buying it. Are you trying anything? Do you need me to watch Roly?" Roly was Laurie's name for the baby, short for Roly-Poly. Laurie eyed the items Mary had slung over one arm.

"Sure. Go ahead and change, and as soon as you come out I'll go in."

Laurie returned to the dressing room and admired the dress in the mirror one more time before changing into her own clothes.

She pushed her godson's stroller around the store and checked out the furniture section. There were a few pretty items, but nothing she was interested in buying for the house on Evergreen.

Finally Mary caught up with her. "So your dress is taken care of. What's Chase wearing for the wedding?"

Laurie let out a sigh. "The same suit he wore to Alice's funeral. Same one he wore to Jenny's funeral." Jenny was Chase's late wife.

"Want to look for something for him? It's not too late," Mary said.

"Maybe I can find a different suit at the Treasure Chest. Or at least a new shirt and tie. I'll probably stop in there tomorrow and check out that evening bag you mentioned."

As the two stood in line with their items, Laurie glanced into a long glass case filled with jewelry and other small valuables.

"Looking for some earrings to wear with the dress?" Mary asked. "You don't own much jewelry, do you."

"Actually I was looking to see if there were any little keys in there."

"You're serious about wanting to get into that box," Mary said. "Just remember, it doesn't belong to you."

"Oh, I know. I'm just inquisitive," Laurie said.

"Nosy," Mary said, disguising the word in a fake cough.

"May I remind you, I did get an 'A' in my investigative reporting class in college," Laurie said.

"I'm sure you did."

Chapter 7.

There was little investigative reporting needed when it came to covering the news in Chinkapin. Everyone seemed to think their holiday events were newsworthy. People always liked to see their picture in the *Journal*, as long as it wasn't in the police blotter.

On Tuesday Laurie found two submissions in her inbox, sent in by eager subscribers hoping their stories would be published. One was about a church pageant, and the other covered a holiday concert at the middle school. If they took the trouble to send in the information with photos, Laurie obliged by providing a little polish and forwarding the stories to Scott. The news was never earth-shaking, but the articles were popular.

Laurie finished editing a piece on a Christmas play at the Chinkapin Methodist church and switched off her desk lamp. She was tired of all the hoopla. It just didn't feel like the Christmas season, even though everywhere she turned there were signs of the holiday. The city had hung out its time-worn decorations on utility poles throughout town. There was even a display of lighted snowmen (snowmen!) in front of the courthouse. The weather was cold and damp, but there were no lovely snowflakes in the air. Things still looked too green.

She needed some cheering up, and took herself to the only place she could think of that was guaranteed to lift her spirits.

The door of the Coffee Pot café was too steamy to see through, but as Laurie pulled it open the smell of freshly ground coffee filled her nostrils as always. She inhaled deeply and smiled at a fat brown gingerbread man in the bakery display case.

Someone called her name, and Laurie was less than thrilled to see Jeff Williams wave her over to his table.

"Just the person I wanted to see," he said. "I have that photo of the dog you asked Sharon to paint. There's something I wanted to ask you."

Laurie's heart sank. She knew Jeff was a fast painter when he needed to be, but it was getting close to Christmas and Laurie wanted her gift for Chase to be perfect, and ready on time.

"You haven't started it yet?" she asked.

"Oh, yeah. I've started it." Jeff picked up his phone from where it lay beside his cup of black coffee. He swiped the screen and handed it to Laurie.

From what she recalled of the photo of Chase's dog Beebee, the likeness was amazing. She couldn't pull her eyes away from the image. "That's coming along great! How big is it, again? I can't tell from your phone."

"It's sixteen by twenty. I didn't know how you planned to frame it, but that's a popular size. It shouldn't be hard to deal with. Of course we do custom frames in my shop."

Laurie barely heard him as she examined the painting again. "Are you going to put something in the background?"

"That's what I wanted to ask you. In the photo there's some stuff near the dog. Wait." He pulled a small notebook from the pocket of his jacket, and withdrew the photo of Beebee. "I was actually on my way to the Treasure Chest to look for you. Look here." He indicated some items in the photo. "Do you know if any of these are special toys of Beebee's? I wanted to include something in the background, but didn't want it to be just random."

Laurie was surprised by Jeff's thoughtfulness. She tried to remember what Chase had told her about his pet. "There." She pointed to a small item in the corner of the photo. "He said Beebee had a toy squirrel almost as big as she was that she dragged around everywhere. I think that's it."

Jeff looked closely at the photo. "A squirrel it is. That shouldn't be too hard. Thanks."

"I'm glad you found me," Laurie said. She felt like she should be nice to Jeff, since he was obviously trying to do a good job on her painting. "So, um, how's business at your gallery?"

"Terrific. Almost more than I can handle. Plus I've picked up a side line. People bring in old paintings and, for a fee, I check them out and tell them whether they're valuable. Weird, huh?"

"Yeah. I can't imagine," Laurie said, remembering the incident with Jeff and the Winslow Homer painting.

"And I never advertised it as a service or anything. It just sort of happened organically."

"Well, if it helps the bottom line, I say go for it." Laurie shrugged, and looked around for a way to extricate herself. "So, when do you think the painting will be finished?"

"Depends on what you mean by 'finished.' I'll be done painting it before the end of the week. If you want it framed it'll take just a little longer. I've hired an assistant to do some of that work."

Laurie didn't know why she hadn't thought of it before, but it would make a better gift framed. She just hoped that didn't add too much to the price. Her finances were tight as it was. "So what do I do, just come in and look at frame samples or something?"

"Yep. That's all you need to do."

She nodded. "Great. I'll be in soon. Probably the first of next week." She rapped her knuckles on the table. "Look, I've got to grab something and head over to the Treasure Chest. Beautiful work on the painting!"

Running into Jeff wasn't at all what Laurie had hoped for. She had planned to relax with a treat and catch up on her social media feeds. C'est la vie. She had totally forgotten to check in with him, and was glad he was making progress on the painting. Without that, what would she have to give Chase for Christmas?

And thinking of gifts, Laurie made a mental note to pick up a wedding gift for Saturday. She turned her attention back to the bakery case near the counter. She was sure she had seen a gingerbread man in there when she walked in, but now the tray was empty. She ordered a large chestnut praline latte to-go, and resigned herself to a lunch of peanut butter crackers.

Laurie took her coffee to the Treasure Chest, set it on the counter as she entered the shop, and went straight to the display of purses. She found a sparkly silver evening bag, but not the black one Mary had told her about. She was still looking for it when Virginia appeared.

"Hey, Laurie. How are you?"

"Okay, I guess. I was looking for a black evening bag, but I don't see anything like what Mary described. There's just this silver one."

"It's in the office," Virginia said. "Mary called and asked me to set it aside for you."

"Oh, good. Let me have a look." She followed Virginia to the office. "Have you been busy today?"

"Not bad for a Tuesday. Joan and I have been working in the back, but there's no place to put anything with all the Christmas stuff we have out. I wish we could put it all on half price already."

"Why don't you just do it? Just tell people when they come in?"

Virginia lowered her voice. "Because *Evelyn* is also here. I swear, she just came in to keep us from putting things on sale." She started talking normally again. "Anyway, here's the purse."

It was a small black evening bag, nothing over the top, but it had a nice wrist strap, and it was a perfect size for a few items Laurie might want to carry on a date or an evening out.

"Oh, this is perfect. I found a dress yesterday at Thriftique."

"Mary told me. She said it was gorgeous. You need to take a picture of it on, so I can see it. And you're going to that wedding this weekend, right? If you need a gift, I can make you a deal on a beautiful crystal vase we have here. I'm sure we could rustle up a box for it."

"Sounds nice," Laurie said, pondering. She knew it would save her a few dollars, but she shook her head. "I think I'll just go the gift card route. This is not the first time for either of them, and who knows what they might need or want. I'll let them pick something. I'll tell you what I do need is something for Chase to wear. I'd love to get him a new suit, but I'd settle for a nice shirt and tie. Just something different, so he's not wearing the same thing he wore to the funeral a couple of weeks ago."

Virginia started to follow her to the men's clothing room, but stopped to help a customer who had brought some items to the counter. In the hallway Laurie met Evelyn carrying an armload of long-sleeved men's shirts. "Are you putting those out?" Laurie asked, confused because Evelyn was headed the wrong way.

"Oh, these will never sell. I don't know why they bothered to tag them. I'm sending them on to the mission."

Laurie's eyes widened. She followed along as Evelyn strode to the other end of the shop. With her long legs, the woman was hard to keep up with. "Wait," Laurie said. "There are a couple I want to look at. I'm trying to find something for Chase."

Evelyn stopped. "He doesn't need shirts like these to work on heating systems," she said.

How does she know what Chase wears to work? Laurie thought. The two women stared at each other for a moment. Quietly Laurie said, "I just want to look at them."

"Well, here." Evelyn thrust them into her arms. "Put them in the mission box when you're done." She turned and went back the other way.

Laurie closed her eyes and took a deep breath. *Count to ten, Laurie, count to ten.* She opened her eyes again. She held only half a dozen shirts, fewer than she'd thought at first, and a couple of them did look frayed around the cuffs. But one was white with a subtle cranberry stripe in it. She checked the size. It was just right for Chase.

She took the rest off of their hangers, folded them, and put them in the mission box. Then she went back to the men's clothing room to look at neck ties. Virginia soon joined her. "Stay close to me, Virginia," Laurie said quietly. "I think I could murder a certain someone, and I really don't want to spend Christmas in jail."

"Trust me. I know the feeling."

"Look at this shirt. I think it'll go great with Chase's dark suit. Help me find a tie."

As they looked Evelyn went up and down the hallway carrying clothing.

"She's putting all that stuff in the mission box," Laurie murmured, narrowing her eyes. "Why the hell do we spend time tagging clothes if she's just going to come around behind us and give the stuff away? At least wait until the end of winter! Give people a chance to buy things, for cripe's sake!"

"It burns me too," Virginia said. "She's got this idea that if things are not new enough or 'in-style' enough for her divine bod, than no one is going to buy them. I wish she would learn that other people can't afford to be as picky as she is. But it's not worth getting upset about, unless you're willing to quit over it, or to have her quit. It's not like we're mobbed by people who want to volunteer here."

Laurie remembered what Mary had told her: that Evelyn didn't want Virginia to work at the shop anymore, and was trying to get rid of her. Virginia was one of the few volunteers from outside of St. Mark's. And as often as they asked other members of the church to volunteer, it was difficult to get anyone to commit to a regular schedule. It was helpful when someone came in and priced items, tagged clothes, or worked the counter for an hour or two, but what they really needed were volunteers they could count on. It had gotten harder to keep the shop open four days a week. They couldn't afford to have anyone drop out.

"This one," Laurie said finally. "What do you think?" She held a tie up next to the shirt.

"Yeah, that'll work." Virginia nodded. "Looks nice."

"I think so too. If you'll write up the ticket, I'll just check out and leave you guys to it. I've got enough stress in my life without coming here and being aggravated."

They returned to the check-out counter, and Virginia wrote up the sales ticket. Laurie handed over the cash and glanced through the door as she waited for her change. "There are a bunch of cars in the church parking lot. Do you know what's going on over there?"

"Yeah, Anne and a couple other people were here earlier. They said something about rummaging around the church for Christmas decorations, or straightening up or something." Virginia lowered her voice again. "I keep hoping Evelyn will go join them."

"Poor you," Laurie said. "If you want, I can arrange for someone to call her from an unlisted number and tell her that her house is on fire." She wiggled her eyebrows.

"Go for it!" Virginia smiled. "You'd be doing me a favor."

"Bye. I'm going next door to see what's going on."

Chapter 8.

Laurie stashed her purchases in the trunk of her car and entered the church kitchen though the back door. She almost ran into Anne, carrying a bucket of water smelling faintly of bleach. "Hi, Anne. What's going on?"

Anne heaved the bucket up on the counter and poured the water into the kitchen sink. "Cleaning," she said. "Trying to get everything in shape for Christmas. I've been going over the nursery with Cathy."

"What happened to the regular cleaning service?" Laurie asked. "I thought they came every week."

"They only do so much. They mop the floors and clean the bathrooms and do some dusting, but anything else is up to us. Every once in a while we just have to do more. I figure we'll get some visitors over Christmas, and we don't want them to be grossed out."

Laurie nodded. "I'm surprised Evelyn isn't over here helping."

"She came early and worked some in the parish hall, but then I guess she decided to tidy up at the Treasure Chest."

"Yeah, she's working over there." Laurie decided to keep her thoughts to herself about whether Evelyn's tidying up at the Treasure Chest was really necessary. Cleaning and scrubbing weren't Laurie's favorite sports. She wondered if she could claim a prior engagement and slip out of the church without much notice. Anne provided another option.

"The parish hall is done, and Cathy and I just about finished with the kitchen and nursery. Maybe you can help Carol. She's working somewhere in the office wing."

"I'll go see how she's doing." Laurie wandered up the hall following the sound of a shredder.

The church offices occupied a small wing that included the rector's and secretary's offices, a vestry, and a small library; really just a jumble of books on a couple of shelves. Carol was attempting to straighten them out. Laurie found her standing in front of the empty shelves with stacks of books arranged around her on the floor. Mother Barbara was rummaging through a file cabinet in the office beyond.

Laurie tapped gently on the door frame.

Carol looked over her shoulder. "Well hey, Laurie, how are you?"

"I'm fine. I didn't want to startle you. I was afraid you'd knock over one of your stacks and then the whole place would come down like dominoes."

"I've kind of got these sorted in order, if you can help me put them on the shelves." She explained how she had sorted them, and she and Laurie got busy re-shelving the books so members of the parish could find what they wanted to borrow.

As they worked Laurie decided to feel Carol out with regard to Virginia. "I was glad to see Virginia next door. She helped me find the perfect tie for Chase to wear this Saturday."

"That's nice," Carol said.

"Plus she made sure the little handbag I wanted was set aside for me."

"Virginia is a real help over there."

Laurie nodded, satisfied. "This is much better," she said when they'd got the books up off the floor. "What about the stuff in this box over here?" she asked.

"Those are a couple of tattered Bibles, and some fiction that doesn't really belong. Everything in the box is going over to the Treasure Chest."

Laurie bent to look through the books while Carol swept the small library with a broom.

"Fore!" a voice called out. "I don't want to hit you on the head with this." Mother Barbara held a basket containing more items to be added to the box.

"Anything interesting?" Laurie stood to peek into the basket.

"Bits and bobs. Free tablets of notepaper, old binders, a paperweight that would be lethal if it hit you; it was left by my predecessor. There are a few random office supplies, and items I have no earthly use for. Might as well try to flog them next door."

Laurie watched as Barbara placed them one by one into the box. "Hey, what's that?" she cried suddenly. She reached out her hand, and Barbara dropped a key into her palm.

"Isn't this pretty," Laurie said. The little key was suspended from a gold chain. The top was decorated with scrolled arms that met to form a heart shape which enclosed a crown. The chain looked like it might be gold, but the key itself was a dull brass. "What does it go to?"

"I have been asking that question ever since I came here. I found it stuck in the front page of an empty photo album."

"Hmmm," Laurie mused. "Probably it went to something that was thrown out or replaced a long time ago."

"That was my conclusion," Barbara agreed. "It's not for the ambry. My next thought was that it opened something in the sacristy, but the altar guild assures me it does not. No one else had a clue, and heaven knows I've tried it on every other lock I can think of."

"I saw some really pretty little keys similar to this in the pawn shop last weekend. They were going for five and ten dollars."

"That's why I put it in the box to go next door. If nothing else, the chain is worth a few dollars."

Laurie nodded thoughtfully.

"Mother Barbara, I'm about to abandon ship," Carol said, purse in hand. "We've done as much as we can here in the library, and I assume you don't want anyone else to touch your office."

"That would be right!" Barbara assured her emphatically. "I have my own unique organizational system, and I'd prefer that no one tried to fix it for me."

Carol laughed. "Well, Laurie, do you want to draw straws to see who takes this box over to the Treasure Chest?"

"I'll take it. I haven't put in the time over here that everyone else has."

"All right, I'll see you Sunday. Have a good evening."

"I'd better get across the parking lot before they close," Laurie said to Barbara. "But I have a question, since this'll be my first Christmas here. I saw the announcement in the bulletin about the greening of the church. Every other place in town has been all winter-wonderland since the day after Thanksgiving. Why do we wait so late to decorate?"

Mother Barbara put a hand on her hip. "All appearances to the contrary, we're still in the season of Advent. The greening of the church shouldn't happen until after the fourth Sunday. Now it depends when that Sunday falls on the calendar. I hate it when Christmas is on a Monday, because that means we have the Sunday service in the morning and have to turn right around and hold the Christmas Eve services that night. But that's not a problem this year since the holiday falls on a Wednesday. So we'll decorate that Sunday evening. The flower guild and altar guild take the lead on that, thank heaven. Since I've been rector here they've always done a beautiful job. All I have to do is offer moral support and bring a couple bottles of wine. You know we usually make it into an event, and have some cheese and crackers, and whatever refreshments people want to bring."

"That's what Mary told me," Laurie said. "Sounds like fun. Well, see you soon." She hoisted the box as Barbara held open the door for her.

Laurie trudged across the parking lot, halting halfway to adjust her load. The books in the box made it surprisingly heavy. Virginia must have seen her on the way over, because she held the shop door open. "Did you find some more treasures for us?" she asked.

Laurie heaved the box onto the counter. "This is all from the library and Mother Barbara's office. Mostly books and office supplies, but look at this." She reached into the box and held out the key suspended from the chain.

"I wonder why that was over there," Virginia said.

"Mother Barbara said she's tried every lock and asked everyone, but it doesn't seem to belong to anything. I've been noticing keys lately. I bought an interesting one at Top Dog the other day, and I saw some in the pawn shop too."

"Well, I think we should sell the necklace separately, don't you?"

"Yeah, I agree. Actually I'd like to buy the key, if you want to price it for me."

"What were they going for at the other places?" Virginia asked, getting ready to write on a sales slip. When Laurie told her the pawn shop's prices Virginia's eyebrows shot up. "Wow! Well, this one's pretty, but it's not ... It's not silver or anything, is it?" She trotted across to the staff kitchen and brought back some polish.

Laurie took it from her and rubbed some silver polish on the key.

"Hmmm," Virginia said. "That looks like brass. So I'd say that's a two dollar key, maybe? What do you think?"

"Two dollars works for me. Write me up."

Virginia wrote up the sales ticket while Laurie washed her hands. Then she dug in her wallet and handed over a few bills.

"How's everything looking at the church?" Virginia asked.

"Nice. Tidy. All that junk in the corner of the parish hall has disappeared. I worked with Carol in the office wing, so the library looks better too. How about over here? Is ...?" Laurie cocked her head in the direction of the back of the shop. She saw Joan coming toward them in the hallway.

Virginia guessed Laurie was asking about Evelyn. "She left about thirty minutes ago." A playful smile broke over her face. "Then Joan and I fetched a few things out of the mission box and put them back on the sales floor."

"You didn't!" Laurie was surprised at her friend's chutzpah.

"Oh yes we did," Joan said. "Listen, dear, I'm not going to bust my hump sorting and tagging things just to have Her Majesty send them straight down to the mission. We should give our customers a chance, at least!"

"Hey, I'm with you," Laurie said.

Chapter 9.

Laurie felt only a little guilty the following Saturday. Chase got up early to put in an hour with whoever showed up to spruce up the church yard, but she was determined to stay home and give herself a beauty break. She knew Mother Barbara would bring doughnuts and make coffee for the workers, so she fixed herself and Chase a light breakfast, sent him on his way, and went up to her apartment.

She fired up her coffee pot, spread a clay mask on her face, and started on her manicure and pedicure. When her nails were almost dry she texted Chase to see how things were going. He answered almost immediately.

A few guys here - trimming and clearing brush. Next we'll tackle the courtyard

She felt better knowing he had help. She didn't like trimming trees and shrubs and hauling brush around. She thought for a moment about the yard she and Chase would have when they moved into their new house. Luckily it was already landscaped. It was just a matter of maintenance. Lord knew there would be enough of that, but she'd seen so many trucks driving around town loaded up with lawnmowers and weed-eaters, she figured a lawn service couldn't be that expensive.

Laurie took a long hot shower, letting the conditioner soak into her hair while she shaved her legs. When she finished she wrapped herself in a fluffy robe and sat on the edge of the tub to look at a few photos Chase had just texted her.

The pictures showed the front of the church and the columbarium courtyard. Everything did look nice when it was weeded and mulched.

Laurie zoomed into one picture and read the names on the plaque in the courtyard. Alice's was the latest, and before hers were other names that sounded familiar: Bynum, Thigpen, Riley, Warren, Barrett, Fordham, Giles, Powers, Gayle. They were names of parishioners she had heard others talk about or seen pictures of. Two she knew belonged to the families of rectors who had served there: Giles and Thigpen. She had seen their photos in the rector's office.

Her phone dinged and a new text from Chase appeared saying he was on his way home. She sent a message back telling him to let her know when he was ready to leave for the wedding. She wanted to surprise him with her new outfit. She wasn't worried about lunch. She certainly planned to eat her share of wedding cake, and whatever else they had at the reception. It was time to get a move on and dry her hair.

She put on her new dress and twirled, trying to see how it swirled in the mirror over the bathroom sink. She hated the thought of having to wear a coat or jacket over it, but then remembered the lovely shawl she had unpacked a few months ago from one of the boxes her brother had brought down from Ohio.

She slipped on her black pumps and stuffed a few necessary items into the evening bag. Chase texted that he was ready any time she was, so she walked down the stairs and knocked on his door.

The smile on Chase's face when he saw her standing in the hall in the velvet dress made all the effort worthwhile. Laurie smiled back, happy to see him dressed up for a change. "You sure cleaned up well. I picked a nice shirt and tie for you, didn't I," she said.

"I can't believe you found that dress in a thrift shop. You look gorgeous." He took her gently in his arms and crooned a few lines from "The Way You Look Tonight." Then he kissed her, careful not to mess her make-up, and offered her his arm. "Ready to go?"

"I'd go anywhere with you."

For the first time in days, the weather was clear and sunny. A lot of leaves had fallen from the trees, and the woods were more open. The scenery looked different since the last time Laurie had driven to Peach Valley.

They were among the first to arrive at St. Michael and All Angels Church. The building of red brick with white trim had obviously been added to over the years. A large parish hall, offices, and other rooms sprawled out to one side.

They parked in back and walked around to enter by the main door.

It was quiet inside. Laurie was struck immediately by the beautiful stained glass window on one side of the church depicting an angelic warrior, sword raised high over his head, ready to thrust it into the serpent under his feet. Organ pipes decorated the wall opposite the window. Otherwise, the church was very plain, with creamy plaster walls and a few smaller, multicolored gothic windows. Choir stalls faced each other at the front of the church. Large white bouquets stood on stands at the back of the sanctuary, and a shining golden cross and white candles stood on the altar.

Laurie looked around nervously. "I don't remember which side is supposed to be the bride's side and which is the groom's. Then again, I'm not sure where we would fit in. I guess I knew Luke before I met Cory."

"That would be this side then." Chase led her to a pew on the right, about halfway up the center aisle.

"You're a man of many talents. How do you know these things?" Laurie asked, sliding into the pew.

"I have a past." He raised his eyebrows at her. "And I've been a groomsman and had to help usher a couple of times. Weren't you ever a bridesmaid or a flower girl or anything?"

"I was a bridesmaid in my sister's wedding. And I was Mary's maid of honor. There wasn't much to it, though, other than to make sure her little train was straight and hold her bouquet. Did you have to hold onto wedding rings or anything?"

"Yep. I never lost a ring, despite the pounding headache I had from the bachelor party."

"Do you suppose Luke and Cory partied last night?" Laurie asked.

"They're probably old fuddy-duddies like us," Chase said. He took Laurie's hand and smiled. "I'd rather party with my bride-to-be the night before the wedding anyway, and get the honeymoon started early."

"I like that idea."

The nave grew livelier as someone propped open the door and more people filed into the church. An usher handed a service leaflet to Laurie. She read it through, and picked up the prayer book to find the celebration and blessing of a marriage. Chase looked over her shoulder.

She pointed to one of the prayers to be read after the marriage ceremony. "It says '... that each may be to the other a strength in need, a counselor in perplexity, a comfort in sorrow, and a companion in joy.' Have I been a 'counselor in perplexity' to you?"

"I remain perplexed. It would take more than a counselor to un-perplex me." He tugged the book from her hands. "Anyway, it says 'that each *may* be,' future tense, so I guess there's hope that you may yet un-perplex me." He continued looking at the prayers. "So you've never told me whether you want to write your own vows, or anything. I hear you're pretty good at writing."

Laurie scrutinized his expression, trying to guess whether he was just being playful or was serious. "Why write something new when I like what's already in the prayer book? Like 'Those whom God has joined together let no one put asunder.' Despite my divorce, I still love this stuff. Keeping in mind this book was updated in, what, the 1970's? It's like the house we're buying. I'm glad the electrical system has been updated, but some of the traditional stuff is the prettiest."

"So you want that scripture reading about wives being subject to their husbands?" Chase had a wicked smile on his face.

Laurie punched him hard on the arm.

"Ow!" A few people turned in their direction, and Chase lowered his head trying to be inconspicuous. "Kidding! Just kidding," he said rubbing his arm.

"Keep it up pal. I'm sure I can take this ring back to the pawn shop for a full refund."

"I'll leave the readings up to you then. But we still have to decide on the hymns and all the music. Can I have a little input there at least?"

"Maybe," Laurie said. "Of course my 'wedding consultant' has provided plenty of suggestions."

Chase laughed. Since Mary was full of advice for every aspect of Laurie's life, he knew their wedding would be no different.

As they chatted, the organist took her seat at the console at the front of the church and began to play a Bach adagio. People who had lingered at the back of the church scrambled to take their seats. The bride's and groom's families were seated by the ushers in the front of the nave.

Luke and Father Callaway, the rector of St. Michael's, entered the church from the side door and stood at the end of the aisle near the single step that led to the choir stalls and the sanctuary. "Check out the suit Luke is wearing," Laurie whispered to Chase. It was brown. His shirt had a stiff-looking high collar, and he wore an ascot tie. Laurie thought the style looked good with his beard and handlebar mustache.

Cory had pressed her sister into being the matron of honor. She now walked rather quickly up the aisle in a knee-length short-sleeved rose-colored shift belted at the waist. Laurie reminded herself that although this was not Cory's first wedding, it was the first for Luke. Some amount of ceremony must have been included for his sake.

Second Home

A moment later the organist brought the prelude to a close and began a traditional wedding march. The crowd in the nave rose and turned to watch.

Cory wore a lacy long-sleeved, knee-length figure-hugging dress, which looked attractive on her curves. Her curly hair was styled in a loose up-do and embellished by a jeweled floral crown. The fragrance of gardenias wafted from her bountiful bouquet. Joy made her appealing face look truly beautiful.

She waved at a few friends on one side of the nave, gave her hand to a woman sitting next to the aisle, and actually laughed at a pair of girlfriends who were bouncing on their toes pumping their fists in victory. Laurie could only hope that she would be as relaxed as Cory looked walking down the aisle.

Then Cory's eyes focused on her groom at the front of the church. He was beaming; the corners of his eyes crinkled upward to match the neatly-waxed ends of his mustache. Cory raised her head proudly, and with a smile that rivaled his own, moved with grace and dignity to join him at the end of the aisle.

"Have you ever seen two people look happier?" Laurie asked Chase.

"Puts a smile on my face just to look at them," he replied.

Father Callaway invited the guests to be seated, and proceeded with the opening of the service. Then in a louder voice he commanded the congregation, "If any of you can show just cause why they may not lawfully be married, speak now; or else for ever hold your peace."

There were a few whispers in the crowd, and someone near Laurie giggled.

Then more quietly the priest said to the couple, "I require and charge you both, here in the presence of God, that if either of you know any reason why you may not be united in marriage lawfully, and in accordance with God's Word, you do now confess it." It was utterly silent in the church.

Father Callaway then addressed everyone in the pews. "Will all of you witnessing these promises do all in your power to uphold these two persons in their marriage?"

Several, like Laurie, were caught off guard, and belatedly responded, "We will." She mumbled to Chase, "I forgot how much audience participation there was in this service."

After more music and prayers came the scripture readings. Laurie was completely surprised when Luke faced Cory and recited the first reading, a selection from the Song of Solomon, from memory.

Second Home

Arise, my love, my fair one, and come away;
For now the winter is past,
the rain is over and gone.
The flowers appear on the earth;
The time of singing has come,
And the voice of the turtledove
Is heard in our land.
The fig tree puts forth its figs,
And the vines are in blossom;
They give forth fragrance.
Arise, my love, my fair one,
And come away.
Set me as a seal upon your heart,
As a seal upon your arm;
For love is strong as death,
Passion fierce as the grave.
Its flashes are flashes of fire,
A raging flame.
Many waters cannot quench love, neither can
floods drown it.
If one offered for love all the wealth of his house,
It would be utterly scorned.

Laurie thought how appropriate it was, considering what the couple had been through before finally arriving at this day.

Cory responded by reciting the next reading, one of Laurie's favorites:

If I speak in the tongues of mortals and of angels, but do not have love, I am a noisy gong or a clanging cymbal. And if I have prophetic powers, and understand all mysteries and all knowledge, and if I have all faith, so as to remove mountains, but do not have love, I am nothing. If I give away all my possessions, and if I hand over my body so that I may boast, but do not have love, I gain nothing. Love is patient; love is kind ...

She continued, her warm beautiful voice filling the nave. By the time she pronounced the ending sentence, "And now faith, hope, and love abide, these three; and the greatest of these is love," Laurie wanted to stand up and cheer. The organist launched into another anthem, and Laurie squeezed Chase's hand.

Finally the couple exchanged their vows. They spoke only to each other, as if unaware of all the friends and family around them. Laurie felt like she was eavesdropping on something private, and lowered her eyes to look at her own beautiful engagement ring.

The priest announced, "Those whom God has joined together let no one put asunder." It seemed like a good place for the organist to play a triumphant anthem, but there were still more prayers and blessings for the married couple. Only when Father Callaway said, "The peace of the Lord be always with you," did they exchange their first kiss as husband and wife. The organist launched into a noisy recessional hymn, and the bride and groom swept down the aisle and out the front door.

"Wasn't that nice?" Laurie said, beaming at Chase. "No eloping for me. I want our wedding to be joyful and beautiful like this. And I want a beautiful new dress!"

"As you wish," Chase said, and lifted her hand to his lips.

Chapter 10.

"The bride and groom invite you to join them in the parish hall for refreshments," Father Callaway announced.

Laurie and Chase followed the crowd down a long hallway past offices and Sunday school rooms to the parish hall. "I guess the wedding party is going to take pictures in the nave, or something?" Chase asked.

"It wouldn't surprise me," Laurie said. "Let's mingle. Maybe we can find some coffee or punch or something." The parish hall was bright and cheery, and actually larger than the nave. Chase went to say hello to the organist, and find out where she had found the coffee she was drinking. Meanwhile Laurie saw Stan Bishop, the editor of the Peach Valley *Register,* across the room, and went over to chat.

"Happy day, isn't it," he said.

"Very happy. It was a beautiful service." She smiled and pointed at Chase. "My fiancé and I have been taking notes."

"Oh, I had no idea. Congratulations."

Chase led the organist over and introduced them, and handed a cup of coffee to Laurie.

The men shook hands and Stan asked, "When's the big day for you?"

"Unfortunately we don't have a good answer for that yet!" Chase said. He looked to Laurie, who shrugged. "In the spring, or maybe a little sooner. We're working on buying a house at the moment."

They all chatted together about the wedding service, the music, and the flowers. The bouquets that were in the sanctuary had been moved to a small buffet table in the middle of the room. A traditional tiered wedding cake stood on a side table, and coffee, tea, and punch were being served just outside the kitchen. A woman set plates of hors d'oeuvres on the buffet.

Finally the bride and groom entered the parish hall and took their places next to the buffet table as guests lined up to congratulate them and help themselves to the food. As Chase and Laurie waited in line, they discussed plans for their own wedding reception. "We could have one big bouquet behind the altar at St. Mark's, and then use it as a centerpiece in the parish hall," Laurie said.

"And have the buffet tables set up perpendicular to each other."

"With tables and chairs around the periphery. That way people could either sit and visit or stand around like at a cocktail party."

"Speaking of cocktail party," Chase looked around, "I guess since this is an afternoon wedding there's no alcohol. That definitely saves money."

"I'd rather pay for a barista than a bartender. Let's have a morning wedding, and keep things simple. I want a nice new dress, some pretty flowers, a beautiful, meaningful ceremony, and a simple reception."

"You mean lunch," Chase corrected her.

"Well, I was thinking just cake, and you probably want sweet iced tea, and a few snacks."

"If by snacks you mean barbecue and all the trimmings."

"You're joking, right?" Laurie said, smiling at him. She saw the serious look on Chase's face and her smile faltered.

"Barbecue is not a joking matter, Laura May," Chase said. "I was thinking of a lunch of barbecued pork, Brunswick stew, maybe a vegetable like mac 'n' cheese or green beans ..."

"Wait, wait, wait. Time out. First of all, macaroni and cheese is not a vegetable. Second of all ..."

Chase's mouth dropped open and he was about to argue with her, but they had reached the head of the receiving line. "Best wishes," Laurie said, shaking Cory's hand. "You look gorgeous today."

"We liked the service, especially the way you two recited the readings," Chase said.

"Yeah," Laurie agreed. "I've never seen that done before. Weren't you nervous?"

"Nervous is for kids," Cory said.

"Speak for yourself," Luke said. "I was nervous. I hope I said everything right."

"If either of you goofed, I'm sure no one noticed. We might just steal those readings for our wedding in the spring," Laurie said.

They moved along so others waiting in line could have their turn. Chase handed a plate to Laurie and took one for himself, and looked over the offerings on the buffet. "Well, we can always go for a burger after we leave here."

"A burger? What are you talking about? This looks great." Laurie put a chocolate-covered strawberry on her plate.

"You can't make a meal out of chocolate-covered strawberries!"

Second Home

"Watch me," Laurie said selecting a second strawberry.

Chase growled. "You weren't the one wielding the hedge trimmer and dragging branches around the church-yard this morning." He heaped his plate with crackers and cubes of cheese.

"Poor darling. Have a cashew." Laurie put a nut on his plate. "As if you didn't probably have two or three doughnuts before lunch."

"I had one doughnut, and I didn't have any lunch."

Laurie raised her eyebrows, and then pouted. "I thought you'd made yourself a sandwich or something." She looked at the refreshments again. There were a few sweet and savory items, and of course the cake, but not what you'd call a meal for a guy who had worked outdoors all morning.

"I'd like to give our guests a real meal at our reception," Chase said.

"You're talking some bucks there, bro," Laurie said. "I hope you're saving up for it. My dad already paid for one wedding reception. He's not going to pay for another."

"Did I say anything about money?" Chase asked. "Maybe I'll do the cooking myself."

Laurie sighed. "I was thinking wedding cake, pastel buttermints, Jordan almonds. Maybe cheese straws, since apparently you can't have any kind of reception in Georgia without cheese straws." She hadn't acquired a taste for cheese straws yet.

"Look, you're happy to eat whatever I cook for you most of the time. Let me worry about food for the wedding. And if you really want a light buffet I suppose Vienna sausages, hoop cheese, and saltine crackers will be just fine."

Laurie stuck her tongue out.

The wedding couple had greeted everyone in line, and moved to cut the wedding cake.

"I hope they don't do the thing with smearing cake all over each other," Laurie said.

"Ooh, I hope they do." Chase moved closer and breathed in Laurie's ear. "I'm planning to smear cake all over your body, and then I'll—"

"Stop!" She squirmed quickly away from him. "Behave yourself!"

A few people turned to stare at them, and Laurie pointed toward the cake, hoping to direct people's eyes away from her blushing cheeks. Then she poked her finger into Chase's ribs. "You smear cake on me at our wedding, and I'll be serving *your* ribs on a platter."

"Feisty! I like a feisty woman." Chase smiled.

* * *

Sunday morning Laurie and the rest of the choir finished their post-service practice and straggled toward the parish hall. They polished off the remaining snacks and drinks and Carol, who had hosted the coffee hour, began cleaning up the kitchen.

"I'm glad I caught you," Laurie said. "I'm conducting an unscientific poll. Chase and I are making plans for our wedding, and I wondered if you could tell me, what is your favorite food to have at a wedding reception?"

Chase was pouring himself a cup of coffee, and lifted his head with interest.

"Favorite food," Carol repeated, her brow furrowed, deep in thought. "Well, I guess I'd have to say cheese straws."

Chase had just taken a sip of coffee and started coughing violently. Laurie saw the smirk on his face, and eyed him sourly. "Don't choke there, buddy," she said flatly, and turned back to Carol. "Cheese straws, huh? Well thanks for that suggestion." Through the corner of her eye she watched Chase still smiling as he headed to the parish hall.

Laurie lowered her voice to ask about the rumor that was still circulating concerning Evelyn wanting Virginia "fired." Carol was the volunteer committee chair, but Laurie knew she didn't like to make waves, and didn't want to be on Evelyn's bad side, which seemed like all sides to Laurie.

"No one's going to be fired," Carol assured her. "I like Virginia. Everyone else does too. Evelyn thinks she gets her way all the time, but she doesn't really. I know she 'rearranges' and hides things at the Treasure Chest, so we move them back around when she's gone. You just have to know when to ignore her."

Laurie remembered the tropical watercolor Evelyn had stashed in a cupboard at the shop; the same painting that was worth well over a million dollars. "Sometimes it's hard to ignore a thorn in your side, though."

Chapter 11.

Laurie had put it off as long as she could, but on
Monday she decided she'd better pay a visit to Jeff's
gallery. She didn't see a way to avoid it if she was going to pick out a frame for the painting she'd commissioned. From the photo he had texted her over
the weekend, the finished artwork was perfect. So
after she got off work, she parallel-parked her old
Malibu on Commerce Street in front of Williams
Gallery and Frame Shop.

The big display widow was rimmed with Christmas lights, and held several paintings showing win-
tery scenes of ice skaters and families hiking through
the snow to find just the right Christmas tree. *Of
course there's no snow within two hundred miles of
here, but some things are sacred*, Laurie thought.

She pushed open the door and tapped the bell on
the counter. The hammering coming from the back
room stopped abruptly, and a moment later a straw-
berry-blonde in skinny jeans and a tight mohair

sweater rounded the corner, tack hammer in hand. "Hey. How can I help you?"

"Jeff just finished a painting for me, and I need to pick a frame."

The woman furrowed her brow. "Which one ... well, just come on back. He brought three paintings by earlier this morning."

Laurie stepped through the doorway and into the workshop. There were framed paintings on the walls, unframed paintings propped on easels, and one face-down on a workbench. "Wow! Are all of these Jeff's?" There were over a dozen in all, but as Laurie looked she realized they were executed with varying degrees of skill, and a few were of the same scene.

"Some are, and some were done by students." The blonde flipped through a stack of canvasses. "I'm sorry, what was your name again?"

"Laurie Lanton. It's a picture of a little dog."

"I found it." She pulled out the painting of Bee-bee. "Let's go to the front and you can pick a frame."

The woman set it carefully on the counter, and pointed to the wall behind her where samples of picture framing materials were stuck to a display board with Velcro. "I can make some suggestions, but did you have something in mind? Wood? Metal? Rustic or more formal?"

The women spent the next five minutes checking out frame samples held up to the painting, and finally Laurie picked the one she liked best, a medium-brown pecan wood which brought out some of the colors in the painting.

"Once it's framed we'll text you a picture, and then have it wrapped and ready for you to pick up. All you'll have to do is add some Christmas paper and a bow." The blonde smiled, and suddenly Laurie realized why she looked familiar. She was one of the women Laurie saw the first time she'd attended one of Jeff's painting classes. As Laurie recalled, the woman had been flirting hard.

As Laurie paid for the painting she said, "You're a painter yourself, aren't you?"

"I do framing and some painting. Actually I've done more artist's modeling," she answered.

Laurie nodded and smiled. *I'll bet*, she thought. *Probably in the nude.*

Laurie treated herself to lunch at the Coffee Pot, thanked her lucky stars again that she had not gotten romantically involved with Jeff, and strolled up Main Street for a little more Christmas shopping.

* * *

That evening Laurie found Chase in his apartment spreading pizza dough on the baking stone he had bought recently at the Treasure Chest. He sang a dramatic aria from "Pagliacci" as he spread tomato sauce on the dough. He topped it with chopped mushrooms and bits of cooked sausage, and then covered the whole pizza with a generous layer of grated cheese.

He stopped singing abruptly. "And now we put her in the oven." With a flourish he opened the door to the hot oven and slid the pizza inside. They enjoyed a glass of red wine while the pizza baked.

"I found a Christmas present you could buy me," Chase announced with a mischievous look on his face.

"You did!" Laurie paused in the middle of swirling the wine in her glass.

"Don't you want to know what it is?"

"Of course," she said. *Not really*, she thought. The beautiful painting of Beebee faded a little in her mind.

"They've got a Martin D-28 in the pawn shop. I checked it out this afternoon. It's in great shape, like someone bought it and just had it put away for years."

Laurie had no idea what he was talking about. Her face must have betrayed her, because he added, "It's a guitar."

"Well, sure it is," she said, irritated. "What does something like that usually go for?"

"Normally, a lot more than what he's asking, but Barry's willing to make a deal on it." Chase quoted her the price.

Laurie's eyes widened. "Is that good?"

She and her ex had split the proceeds from the sale of their house and furniture up north, and Laurie had tried not to touch the money since she'd moved to Georgia. Lately it was disappearing fast. Some of it was going as part of the down payment on their new house. She had hoped to save the rest of it to buy furniture, and a new outfit for her wedding.

"It's too good to pass up. I need to make a decision today and let him know. What do you say, Santa-baby? The pawn shop is open until seven." Chase looked at her with an eager smile, and Laurie thought how cute he was. Not handsome, but appealing. She had to smile in spite of herself.

"Well," she drew it out playfully. "I don't know. You have been a *fairly* good boy this year."

"You want to see just how good I can be?" He put his arms around her and pulled her close.

Suddenly Laurie had a flashback of her ex, who had been known to withhold affection when he didn't get what he wanted. DB had all kinds of ways to manipulate people, and Laurie had been naïve enough to fall for most of them and never see what hit her.

She scowled as she wiggled out of his arms and turned away.

"Hey!" Chase sounded hurt. "Look, it's not a big deal," he said. "I thought I was being helpful. I'm kinda clueless what to get *you* for Christmas, and I thought you wanted to know what I wanted."

"Sorry. I haven't been in much of a Christmas mood."

Chase pulled the pizza out of the oven, and they pointedly avoided any discussion of Christmas or presents as they ate their meal. But Laurie felt guilty. She was sure that Chase would have dropped the whole idea, but after they cleaned up the dishes she led him across the parking lot to the pawn shop. He went straight to the musical instruments and reached for the guitar.

She could tell as Chase played a few riffs that he really wanted it. It had a mellow, powerful tone. "It's just a decent, popular model. A good acoustic guitar. I can use it for teaching too. Although I haven't done much of that lately." Chase hadn't had much time for teaching, and hadn't even done much song-writing in the last month. Laurie hoped that would change once they got past the holidays, and moving, and the wedding. Come to think of it, would things ever settle down?

"You wouldn't be able to touch it until Christmas," she said. He nodded happily. The longer Chase handled the guitar, the more certain she was that it was the right gift for him. And the more she regretted commissioning the painting.

* * *

Laurie parked outside the Treasure Chest Tuesday afternoon and pulled her hood up against the light rain. The bells jangled on the glass as she ducked inside and wiped her feet on the mat.

Mary looked up from making change for a customer. "Hi, Laurie. Come in and get that wet jacket off."

"I was just watching the rain out there," the customer said. "I guess I'll have to dash to my car." She was a short, older woman with graying hair arranged in neat waves. Laurie thought the woman probably couldn't "dash" anywhere even if the building were on fire. "Do you have any umbrellas for sale?"

"I'm sorry, no," Mary said. "I do have a rain bonnet, though. Would you like it?"

"Yes please. And how much do I owe you for it?"

"On the house," Mary called, rummaging in the office and finally handing the woman a neatly folded item made of thin plastic. "It's lost its packaging along the way, but you can tell it's never been used."

The woman pulled open the accordion-folded hat, arranged it on her head, and slid her package off the counter. "I thank you very much. You ladies have a nice day, now," she said, and walked with a measured pace out to her car.

"When was the last time you even heard about a rain bonnet, let alone saw someone wearing one?" Mary said returning to the office. "I pulled that thing out of a box earlier today and thought 'what am I going to do with this?' Now I know!"

"Sometimes things appear just when you need them," Laurie said. She shed her jacket, hung it on the coat tree and glanced around. "Who else is here today? Is that Evelyn's purse?"

"Yep."

"Ooh, good thing she didn't see you give away that rain bonnet," Laurie said in a near whisper. "It was probably an antique. We could have sold it for five dollars." She and Mary exchanged a smile, and

Laurie returned to her normal voice. "Boy, that hymn went on forever on Sunday. Why did Steve make us sing the whole thing?"

"Which hymn?" Mary was having difficulty with a tagging gun, and hadn't been paying attention.

"O Come O Come Emmanuel."

"Oh, right. It does go on forever. And it's not my favorite. Seems like we have to do it every year, though. You'd think he could pick something different for a change."

"Have you got most of your Christmas shopping done? Do you have trouble buying presents for Pete?"

"If I get him something it's usually a gag gift. He picks most of his presents for himself."

"Yeah? And he's okay with that?"

"He prefers it that way! How am I supposed to know what kind of golf junk he wants? I have no clue what most of that stuff is, and don't want to know." Mary got that devilish grin on her face. "Plus that way I can pick a few nice things for myself, and he can't say anything. Have you been shopping for Chase? Or are you just going with the painting?"

"Oh, I have to show you what it looks like. It's finished, and it's being framed. I picked the frame out yesterday." Laurie fished her phone out of her purse, found the image, and handed the phone to Mary.

"Aww, cute! He's going to love that."

"And I got Chase's snapshot back." Laurie dug the old photograph of Beebee out of her purse and held it up next to the image on her phone. "Look."

"It's perfect." Mary held them closer for a better look. "If anything the painting is more lifelike and alive-looking."

"I'm tickled with it. But here's the thing. Chase and I had agreed to keep things low-key this Christmas, remember? But then he went and found himself a guitar at the Chinkapin pawn shop that he wanted me to buy for him."

"What does he need another one for? Did something happen to his old guitar?"

"No," Laurie said, exasperated.

"Well, did you buy it for him?" Mary asked.

"Yes." She heaved a great sigh. "He gave me those puppy-dog eyes again. He knows I can't resist him when he does that." Laurie smiled in spite of herself.

"Well, better get used to it. Pete keeps buying golf clubs. I don't know how many he has now, but way more than anybody really needs. I mean, I don't think you need to let golf clubs rest between rounds, or anything."

"Only trouble is I'm running out of cash." Laurie folded her arms. "I have money, but I was saving it for other things, like a dress for my wedding."

"We could go back to Georgia Thriftique," Mary suggested. "They had a lot of nice dresses, remember?"

"I don't know. I had wanted to get something brand new for a change."

As usual, there was a rush of customers late in the afternoon. People tended to stop in around the time they went to pick up kids at school. Laurie and Mary waited on them, and even Evelyn came out of the back of the shop to help.

A young woman brought a pair of black slacks and a couple of blouses to the counter. "I need some things with long sleeves that I can wear to work. It gets so cold there, and I'm sure people get tired of seeing me in the same old shirt and pair of pants all the time."

Laurie nodded. "I hear you. At one place I worked I made a sign for my cubicle that said 'One day I will be in charge of the thermostat.'"

"Yeah, that would be nice. They keep our thermostat locked in a cage."

Laurie took the clothing off the hangers while Mary wrote up the sale. "Is there any way you can come down on this?" the woman asked, holding up the five-dollar tag on one of the blouses.

Mary looked at the date on the tag. The blouse had been on the sales floor since October. She exchanged a glance with Laurie, who shrugged her shoulders. "How about ... three dollars?" Mary said.

Evelyn watched out the window as the customer left. Then she turned to Laurie and Mary with a frown. "Look at that car she's driving. If she can drive a car like that, why was she complaining about paying five dollars for that blouse? That blouse was like new, a Chico's. I get sick of these people haggling over prices all the time!"

"We've had that blouse for sale for a few months," Laurie said.

"In a couple of weeks we'll be selling the older clothes for half price anyway," Mary added.

"You're not the one to decide when our items go on sale," Evelyn said, looking down at Mary and jabbing a finger at her shoulder.

Mary started to reply, but Laurie butted in, her hands on her hips and ice in her voice. "Let's think about this car thing for a minute. Why might someone drive an old Cadillac and then worry about how much they were spending at a thrift shop? Maybe it's because they don't have any *muh-nee!*"

Second Home

Laurie had been trying to remain civil around Evelyn, but now that she had started she wasn't about to quit. "Working-class people drive fancy cars because only well-off people with nice cars donate their old ones to charity. Everyone else trades in their cars, or passes them on to their kids, or drives them until the wheels fall off. In case you hadn't noticed, there's nothing resembling a bus in Chinkapin, Georgia. If there were, that woman would probably be riding it."

Evelyn stood with her mouth open, staring at Laurie. Finally she snapped her jaws together in a tight-lipped scowl. "I wasn't talking to you. What would you know about it?"

"I know plenty about it. I hung around a lot of writers and artists and musicians after I graduated from college: brilliant people, hugely talented, who cobbled together a living teaching and playing gigs, or selling a few paintings or poems, and working rinky-dink jobs to make ends meet. And if they had a car it was usually because some well-healed arts-lover made them a good deal on it, or 'sold' the car to them and never worried about collecting any payments. I knew lots of people who lived hand-to-mouth. Everything they owned came from a thrift shop or the Salvation Army or Goodwill. They lived in the parts of town *you* would never even drive through. I know. If you actually talked to some of our customers, maybe you would learn something."

Evelyn walked stiffly around the counter into the office, grabbed her jacket and her purse, and walked to the door. She paused long enough to say, "I'm sure you two know-it-alls can tally the sales and lock up." Without waiting for an answer she pushed through the door and drove off.

"Yeah, Evelyn, come back when you can stay a while," Laurie said under her breath. "Better yet, don't bother." She slid the sign from "open" to "closed" with a bang.

"She would do well to learn a little empathy," Mary said. "But just remember, we have to work with her and go to church with her." Then a smile broke out on her face. "That was us you were talking about, wasn't it? With the Cadillac?"

"Hell, yes, it was us. That was a sweet car, too. I couldn't wait to get in it in the morning and fire up the heated seats, because our apartment was so cold."

"That thing was a gas-guzzler, though." They both smiled, remembering their early days just out of college. "I got so tired of being broke," Mary added. "'Income insecurity' they call it today. It's scary. It makes people do dumb things. Like me going to work with walking pneumonia because I couldn't afford to go to the doctor and couldn't afford to lose a day's pay. And pushing my best friend to marry a guy I suspected deep down was a jerk, because I didn't want her to be broke forever like me."

"Are you talking about me and DB now?" Years ago Mary had assured Laurie that her first husband was a great catch. He turned out to be a philandering, manipulative jerk, but he did have a good income.

"No comment," Mary said. She put her arm around Laurie's shoulder. "Come on, let's shut the lights and count the money so we can get out of here."

Mary walked through the shop turning off lights while Laurie set the thermostat. "Hey, want to go shopping with me tomorrow afternoon?" Laurie asked. "You can help me pick a little something for Roly."

"I'd love to go shopping, but you can get something for Roly right here. Let me show you what we have in the baby room." Mary led her friend down the hall.

Chapter 12.

"Are you completely sick of holiday music, or would go with me to the Chinkapin Playhouse for the 'Home for the Holidays' variety show? I'm going to write it up for the *Journal*." Laurie sat across from Chase and ate another forkful of sweet potato casserole.

"What? When? Do you mean tomorrow?" Chase asked looking startled.

"No, I mean tonight. It's the dress rehearsal. We want to run something about it in tomorrow morning's paper. The story should write itself, really, just a few paragraphs if I take a couple of cute pictures for filler. I don't even have to stay for the whole thing. Why are you looking so worried? If you don't want to go, I can go by myself."

"I think I forgot to tell you something," Chase said, looking sheepish.

"Uh-oh. This feels kinda familiar. What have you forgotten to tell me?"

"That I promised to play at the Coffee Pot on Friday night."

Laurie rolled her eyes. "Forgot, huh?"

"Well, I told you as soon as I remembered. I'm sorry."

"Oh, don't start on me with the puppy-dog eyes!" Laurie had to smile at him. She knew how hard Chase was trying to do better at communicating. "Scott was planning to go tonight, but he came to work this morning with such a bad cold I felt sorry for him and told him I'd do it. I didn't know the Coffee Pot was getting in on the 'Chinkapin for the Holidays' action. It makes sense, though."

"Yeah, they told me they had trouble getting people to play because their regulars are tied up with the show at the playhouse, so I told them I'd come for an hour. But just Friday, not Saturday."

"Are spouses invited?"

"Absolutely! Free lattes for spouses, all they can drink." He relaxed a bit. "I'll go to your thing if you come to mine." He wiggled his eyebrows at her.

"Oh, baby! Now you're talking."

* * *

"Nice little story," Scott said, looking over the short review Laurie had written about the variety show. "Thanks for covering for me. I felt like crap yesterday. I just went home and crashed." His nose was red, and he still sounded like his head was clogged. "Clever the way you slipped in a mention of the live music coming up at the Coffee Pot this evening." He gave her a wry look.

"Did you like that? I'm going to be all holidayed out after Chase's set tonight. How do musicians stand playing the same songs over and over at this time of year? I can hardly stand writing about it. I've had to get my thesaurus out to find synonyms for Christmas, yuletide, St. Nick, Kris Kringle, and what-not. I don't know what you did before I came along."

"Well, we did print a lot more stuff from the police blotter."

"I might have to wear some ear plugs tonight. Or maybe I'll just slip away and pick up Chase's present. All the shops will be open late."

"Are you getting him a puppy?"

Laurie laughed and shook her head. "Close, but no cigar."

Scott was a certified dog-lover, and knew all about Chase's desire for a dog. "Yeah, you're right," he said. "The chemistry between a man and his dog is a magical thing. Chase had better handle that on his own."

* * *

Laurie ordered a peppermint mocha while Chase set up on the small stage at the back of the Coffee Pot cafe. She was reconciled to him playing occasional gigs. He still loved to perform, and Laurie liked to listen.

She blew on the hot mocha and observed the people around her. Some settled at tables to enjoy the music. Others came in for a hot drink and then headed back into the chilly evening. Outside, people sat on benches near the café, strolled up and down the street carrying packages, or just chatted with neighbors under the Christmas lights.

"Laurie! Mind if we join you for a minute?" Chad Houser stood over her table, one arm around the woman beside him, and gestured with his coffee cup. "I don't think you've met my wife, Hilda."

The two women shook hands while Chad dragged an empty chair over from the next table. "I'm glad I caught you. I wanted to talk to you or Chase." He turned in his seat and waved at Chase, who nodded from the stage.

"Like I was saying, I have good news for you two. How would you like to close on your house right after the New Year?"

"Oh, we'd love to," Laurie said. "The sooner the better."

"Well, it would make the owners very happy, and since the appraisal is done and Chase has waived the inspection, things are moving quickly."

"Did you ever find out anything about that wooden box?" Laurie asked.

"I truly don't know how you found it, because the Hinsdales didn't know a thing about it. They must not have used that little room very much. Mr. Hinsdale bought that house from the Rutherfords, but there are no Rutherfords left in the area. So, bottom line, the box is yours."

"I surely was curious when Chad told me about it!" Hilda said. "Especially since the box is locked. That makes it even more intriguing."

"But the owners don't care, so as soon as we can get together with the lawyer and you and Chase sign all the papers, the box and everything else at 501 Evergreen Drive will be yours. Now, I was looking at my calendar, and we've got these dates to work with."

As Chad talked, Laurie jotted a few things in the little notebook she always carried. "I'll ask Chase this evening," she said, "and text you with the date we like. It'll definitely be that Monday or Tuesday."

"And as soon as I hear from you I'll set it up with the lawyer."

"Listen, Chad. Do you and Hilda mind sitting here while I run an errand? I have to go over to Commerce Street and pick up a Christmas present for Chase. I should be back in about five minutes, but if it takes longer I'll need you to stall him for me."

The realtor and his wife agreed, and while Chase played "Silver Bells" Laurie slipped out of the café. Her car was in a nearby parking lot, and since she had spent a lot of time in the neighborhood by now she was able to navigate the back streets to Williams Gallery and Frame Shop despite the fact that Main Street was closed for the holiday event.

She parked out front and dashed into the gallery where the strawberry blonde was waiting on a customer. Tonight the woman was sporting a Santa Claus hat to match her fuzzy white sweater and green striped tights. The look was finished off with some extra tall high heels, making her look like a very well developed elf from Santa's grown-up toy land.

"Hi. I'm here to pick up a painting. You helped me select the frame about a week ago," Laurie reminded her.

"Right. It's in the back of the shop." She counted under her breath as she made change.

"Hey there. I thought I heard a familiar voice." Jeff stuck his head through the doorway leading into the workshop. "It's nice to see you, Laurie. Come on back. I have you all wrapped and ready to go."

"Great. I only have a minute," she said following him into the workshop. "I snuck away from the café. Chase is performing, and I have to get back."

"The painting is right here." Jeff pointed to a stack of bulky rectangles wrapped in craft paper. He flipped through them until he found the one with her name on it, and pulled off the papers taped to the front. "Here's what the finished product looked like." He indicated a photo. "And I just need your signature saying you picked it up."

Laurie set the paper on the workbench to sign it, and then handed it back to Jeff.

"One more thing." Smiling, he pointed overhead where a bunch of mistletoe hung from the light fixture. "It's customary to kiss the artist for good luck in the coming year." Jeff leaned in and placed a hand on either side of her. Laurie took a step back but was blocked by the workbench. The last thing she saw before she squeezed her eyes shut and turned her face away was his blue eyes coming closer.

She was saved when the blonde leaned through the doorway. "Jeff! Mrs. Riley is on the phone about mats and frames."

He backed away with a sigh of regret, and Laurie straightened, rubbing her back where it had pressed against the workbench. She picked up her painting, carried it to the counter, and paid for it while the blonde glared at her. *Don't blame me, sister*, Laurie thought. Her face was bright red as she hurried out of the shop.

A hard knee to the groin might have straightened him out, she thought as she stashed the painting in the trunk of her car. She wondered why good ideas like that always popped into her mind too late. She promised herself that was *the last* time she would have any dealings with Jeff Williams.

Laurie thanked her lucky stars when she got back to the Coffee Pot and saw her parking spot was still available. Chad and Hilda were inside where she had left them, sharing a small coffee. "Mission accomplished," Laurie said. "Thanks for holding the fort."

Chad stood and shook her hand. "We're going to join the throng of revelers outside, and look for something a little more potent to drink." With a final wave in Chase's direction he and Hilda left the café.

Chase finished his set shortly after, snapped his guitar case shut, and came to sit next to Laurie. She quickly filled him in on everything the realtor had said. "I'm so excited." She clapped her hands lightly.

"I'd be more excited if we had some furniture to move into the place," Chase said, and downed the last of Laurie's mocha. "Want to run over and walk through our new house by moonlight?"

"I don't think the moon is out tonight, and anyway, we don't have a key. How are we going to get in?"

"Watch and be amazed," he raised his eyebrows, and tapped the side of his nose with a knowing look.

Traffic noises on Main Street quickly receded as they walked around the block, and Laurie felt her mood lift as they entered the quiet neighborhood. They rated the Christmas spirit in evidence at each house they passed. A family of snowmen graced a lawn near the corner. Multi-colored Christmas lights twinkled and flashed. Across the street, white lights sparkled in the shrubbery, and at another house spotlights illuminated decorated wreaths on the door and windows.

Laurie looked at 501 Evergreen Drive as they came up the walk. "This is going to be fun to decorate," she said. "I still love this porch. And the double doors."

Chase waved a hand over the door, and in a deep voice said, "Open sesame." Then he bent and punched four numbers into the lock box, and a key dropped into his hand.

"Cheater," Laurie said. A moment later they were inside.

They walked from room to room, holding hands and talking about furniture arrangements. She pictured a couch in front of the fireplace. Maybe a pair of couches with a shared coffee table. "I need a bookcase," she said. "I have so many books in boxes. I don't know if I'll put them in the living room or wherever I put my desk."

"I need room for my guitars, and some sort of cabinet for music books and sheet music, plus business paperwork."

"Business paperwork?" Laurie said. "Why would you bring that stuff here?"

"Music business stuff, not HVAC."

"Oh. Right." She nodded.

They returned to the porch and sat on the swing, snuggling together for warmth. "It sure is a pretty view from here. And I love the tall trees. They remind me of home."

"Hey," Chase admonished gently, "this is your home. Or it will be, as soon as we sign all those papers. We'll make a new life here."

She looked up at him as multi-colored lights softened the stern angles of his face. "I am home when I'm with you."

* * *

The week before Christmas there were a lot of schedule changes among Treasure Chest workers as volunteers went on holiday visits or welcomed family returning home. Carol wanted to take her sister and two nieces shopping, so Laurie agreed to work for her at the shop on Saturday.

She looked forward to working with Virginia, who was subbing for Anne. In fact, she was glad to be working with anyone, as long as it wasn't Evelyn. The less time she spent with Evelyn, the better.

After a lavish breakfast of bacon, eggs, and waffles with fruit topping, Laurie loaded dishes into the dishwasher and kissed Chase goodbye. He was going to the new house to put up some shelves and then paint the kitchen. Laurie hoped he would finish around the time she got off work so they could do something fun together.

She should have known something would interfere with her wonderful plans. Shortly after she arrived at the Treasure Chest and greeted Virginia, Evelyn parked in the lot and came through the door. "Can I hide back here with you for a while?" Laurie asked Virginia, who was busy tagging clothes. "Evelyn can watch the counter."

As Laurie pulled a stack of clothes out of one of the bins Evelyn suddenly stood looming over her. "Laurie, someone is trying to reach you. Your phone is making a lot of noise. Why don't you just keep it in your pocket?"

"Sorry. It must be Chase. He's working at the new house this morning." She made a nasty face behind Evelyn's back as she followed her to the front of the shop. In the office Laurie dug her phone out of her purse and saw texts from both Chase and Chad.

As Laurie responded to the messages, she was vaguely aware of activity at the counter. A woman had entered the shop followed by a rather reedy girl in a loose-fitting plaid flannel shirt. The girl sulked, and lounged against the door.

"My daughter needs some maternity clothes," the woman told Evelyn. At the word "maternity" the girl turned and leaned into the wall, knocking her forehead against it a few times. Her mother grabbed her arm. "Donna, stop that!" Laurie looked up to see what was going on.

"I don't want this baby!" Donna said, refusing to face the woman and looking out the door.

"Like it or not, you're having it. Five months and it'll all be over, and you can get on with your life."

"Seven! I told you seven!"

"More like four, but whatever," the woman said under her breath. She forced a smile and looked at Evelyn, who stood behind the counter wide-eyed. "We may be a little farther along than we think. Do you have any clothes that might work for her?"

"You're in luck. We have a lot of great maternity clothes, and they're two for the price of one! Just one dollar an item. You can get three shirts and two pair of pants for five dollars. Come with me Donna."

Laurie could not believe what she was hearing. Was Evelyn really offering to sell items for half price?

"My name is Melinda, by the way," the woman said. "And you've met my daughter Donna."

"Is this her first baby?" Evelyn asked.

"Yes." Melinda heaved a big sigh. "I would have preferred she had waited until she was married. Now her boyfriend has disappeared off the face of the earth, and she says she's giving the baby up for adoption."

"I am," Donna mumbled.

"Well, we'll see about that." Melinda followed Evelyn across the hall, and Donna slouched along behind them. Laurie stepped out of the office and stood at the counter, where she busied herself folding plastic bags and kept her ears open to the conversation.

The room Evelyn led them to served many purposes. Tall clothes racks held an incongruous assortment of prom dresses, formal wear, and maternity clothes, and part of the room was sectioned off with a curtained fitting booth. Evelyn sounded cheerful as she showed Donna the racks of clothes. "You can do this, Donna. Look here. And when the baby comes, if you've made up with the daddy we even have a wedding gown you can get married in."

Is Evelyn actually engaging in friendly banter with customers? Laurie thought. It was so unlike her.

Donna whined as she listlessly pawed through the clothes. Evelyn, who was taller than everyone in the store, reached over and slid a few hangers along the rack and pulled out some of the newer items. "Let's see. You look like a medium. Actually a small, but you'll probably need some growing room. Now isn't this shirt cute? It has tabs on the side that you can move from button to button as you grow, so it'll work all the way through. And here's another. This is a great color for you!"

The girl tried to back away as her mother held some jeans up to her waist. Evelyn pulled a tunic off the rack and passed it to Melinda, who held it over the jeans. She grabbed two other shirts from the rack and held them up for Donna's approval. "Do you like either of these?"

Donna looked a little more interested, pointing to a blouse in a yellow hound's-tooth plaid, and then walked to the rack to look through the rest of the clothes. In a few minutes the three women each held several items.

"That's enough for now, Donna," Melinda said. "We'll just start with these." They returned to the check-out counter.

Laurie grabbed a pen and the pad of sales slips and started to write up the sale as Evelyn pulled the clothes off their hangers. She took Evelyn at her word, and wrote each item up for half price.

"You know, we have a lot of really nice baby things too," Evelyn said. "We often get cribs, strollers, car seats, just about anything you can think of. If you want to leave your number we can call you as we get things in."

"I don't need anything," Donna said. She sounded sulky again. "I'm going to look around." She walked away from the counter.

"Is this your first time in our shop?" Evelyn asked Melinda.

"It is. I've driven by it a million times, and finally decided to stop. We shop a lot at Georgia Thriftique, but Donna has a friend who works there, and she doesn't want anyone to see her buying maternity clothes. She won't be able to hide that belly of hers forever."

Evelyn offered a suggestion. "I remember back in the day when young women would go stay with an aunt or some other relative until after the baby was born."

"We'll see. I'd rather have Donna where I can keep an eye on her. I've been watching her make poor choices for a long time, led astray by that ... *boyfriend* of hers. It's come home to roost with her now. She needs to grow up, and she'd better do it fast. She's made her bed, as the saying goes."

Donna returned and held out a couple of paper-back books. Her mother scowled at her, but then added them to the pile. Evelyn said, "Those are a quarter each."

Trying not to look too stunned, Laurie finished writing up the ticket.

Chapter 13.

They closed up the shop at two o'clock, and added a sign on the door saying the Treasure Chest would be closed until after the first of January. Then Laurie drove over to Mary's house to pick her up and take her to 501 Evergreen Drive.

Mary slipped out her front door as soon as Laurie pulled in her driveway. "Pete just got Ricky down for his afternoon nap. I thought I'd better meet you out here so you didn't wake them."

"Them?" Laurie smiled.

"Yeah. We all had an early morning. If I didn't want to see inside your new house so bad, I'd be taking a nap too. Was it busy at the Treasure Chest today?"

"Yeah, pretty busy," Laurie said, driving down Redding Road toward town. "We sold quite a bit of the Christmas stuff. And I've seen my first true, bona fide, Christmas miracle."

"What?" Mary asked.

"Evelyn sold a bunch of stuff at half price to a pregnant girl and her mom today."

"Christmas stuff? It was all supposed to be half price."

"No, maternity stuff," Laurie clarified. "And some books! Remember how Evelyn reamed me out about giving those books to Cory a couple of months ago?"

"Oh yeah! That's crazy," Mary agreed.

"It was totally surreal. I thought maybe it was because the girl was pregnant."

"I've never seen her go ga-ga over babies or anything, though," Mary said. "She hardly even looks at mine."

"And Joan always says she treats that dog of hers better than she treats her kids. It really makes no sense at all, because it's so unlike her. I was happy to write up the ticket, though. And she wouldn't talk about it either. I started to say something, but she suddenly remembered she had to be somewhere, and ran out of the shop right at two o'clock. Actually let me and Virginia total up the sales unsupervised."

They turned the corner by the courthouse and continued down the street to Evergreen Drive. "Did you even know this neighborhood was back here?" Laurie asked.

Mary shook her head, looking around. "It's a pretty street, though. These houses have been here a while."

Laurie pulled into the driveway behind Chase's truck. She showed Mary around the yard first, and then brought her back to the front porch. "This is really pretty," Laurie said, "but the back porch is screened. I like that a lot."

"Right? Because Georgia."

"And bugs!" they said together.

"Plus the back porch opens right off the kitchen, and has a ceiling fan," Laurie added, leading Mary through the front door.

Upbeat piano jazz floated on the air from the kitchen. Chase was making good progress painting the walls. "You do good work, darling," Laurie said, trying not to get paint on herself as she kissed him. "I definitely prefer this color over the green! It was sort of a celery color," Laurie explained to Mary. "Pretty, but not my dream color."

Mary nodded her approval. "This color reminds me of milky coffee."

"I guess it does! Maybe that's why I picked it."

"These fireplaces are awesome," Mary said as they continued through the house. "It's going to be so cozy! If you ever get any furniture, that is. Seriously, this is a big place. You're going to have to do some shopping."

"Don't remind me. I'm kinda worried about that. Furniture is expensive, and I don't want to buy in haste and regret at leisure, or whatever the saying is."

"You got that right. So take me upstairs!"

Laurie grabbed a flashlight from a kitchen drawer, and led the way. She was pleased as Mary oohed and aahed over everything in the house. Laurie wanted to be her own person, make her own decisions, live life on her own terms ... but she still craved the approval of the people she cared about most.

Mary agreed that the new "bonus" room would make a great master bedroom. "And where's the little room? Where you found the box? I want to see the secret compartment."

They stepped into the room across the hall and Mary looked at the small closet door. "Now I see what you were talking about. I had a hard time picturing this closet over the stairs thing." She walked out in the hallway to look down the staircase. Then she came back in, opened the closet door and ran a hand along the slanting back wall. "Weird. I've never seen anything like it. Instead of a cupboard under the stairs it's a cupboard *over* the stairs." She ran her fingers tentatively across the floorboards. "I'm not feeling anything."

"Here," Laurie said, and handed her the flashlight. "See if you can see the notch at the back."

Mary moved the flashlight back and forth. "Nope. Nada." Then she reached a hand in and felt farther toward the back. Her eyes widened. "Oh! Hold this." She handed Laurie the flashlight and levered the floorboard up with both hands, pulling it out of the closet and setting it on the floor. Then she reached in and withdrew the box.

She lifted it up and down, testing its weight. Then she held the box near her ear and moved it from side to side, listening as the contents shifted. "It's sure not empty. But it's not very heavy, so I'm with you. Maybe letters. Or photographs."

"Or old teabags. I still think it looks like a tea caddy," Laurie said.

"Kinda," Mary agreed. "Where's that key you bought at Top Dog?"

"In my purse. I'll go get it." She ran down to the kitchen and was back up a moment later. "This is it. If it doesn't work, I had another one I got at the church, but I haven't been able to find it. I think it's back at my apartment."

Laurie slotted the end of the key into the keyhole. It slipped in easily. She held her breath and exchanged a look with Mary. Then she tried turning the key. "It won't turn." She twisted back and forth with more force, but it clearly wasn't moving.

"Oh, well. That would have been too easy," Mary said.

"The other key I have is about the same size, but the teeth on it are different. I wish I hadn't left it at home. Oh, well." She fitted the floorboard back in place in the bottom of the closet, and set the box on top. "No need to hide it anymore, I guess."

Mary glanced at her watch. "You have some fun planned for later?" she asked. "Want to come with Pete and me to a concert at the college in Redding?"

"We're going out to supper for a change, since Chase is still painting, and then maybe we'll take a ride to look at Christmas lights around Lake Whatever-it-is, the place that was written up in the paper."

"Watch out! You might just decide you want to celebrate Christmas after all."

* * *

Second Home

Sunday morning Laurie took her usual seat next to Mary in St. Mark's choir loft. "So how was the concert last night?" Laurie asked.

"Awesome. The little orchestra was great, and the soloists were outstanding. I had a hard time not singing along. And how was your evening?"

"That neighborhood around the lake was pretty, but it was crowded. Traffic just crawled. Downtown Redding was nicer. All the trees in the medians were lighted, and lots of people were out strolling. We even took a little horse and buggy ride, just the two of us!"

"Ooh. Sounds romantic."

"It was. Afterwards we went to one of the coffee shops in town, and for a change I got to sit *with* Chase while someone *else* played guitar and sang on the little stage. So now I'm finally in a Christmas mood, but I'm sad that our apartments are so bare."

"All right choir," Steve said, trying to get everyone's attention. "Let's start with some vocal warm-ups. It's the last Sunday of Advent, and we've got lots of singing to do."

"Tell me we're not singing 'O Come O Come Emmanuel' again," Laurie said, opening her bulletin to check the morning's hymns.

"If we are, you can lip-synch the odd-numbered verses and I'll lip-synch the even ones," Mary said, scanning the announcements on the back. "You coming for the greening of the church this afternoon?"

"Wouldn't miss it," Laurie said.

* * *

Laurie had no idea what to expect that evening, or how many people would show up to "green" the church. Mother Barbara had reminded people about the event, but with all the announcements about the mid-week Christmas Eve and Christmas day services, the greening of the church was something of an afterthought.

"Do we have anything to bring? Maybe we should stop for a bottle of wine, or some cheese and crackers? I wish we'd thought of this yesterday," Laurie said as she and Chase got dressed after their afternoon "nap." They had intended to bake some brownies or something to bring with them to the church, but one thing had led to another and they'd found themselves otherwise, and very pleasantly, occupied.

"I think there'll be plenty of that kind of stuff."

Chase looked thoughtful a moment, and in the silence Laurie could hear his stomach growl. She laughed. "Sounds like you could use some real food."

He looked at his watch. "We don't have much time. Let's stop at the Tasty Chick and pick up some chicken tenders. We can cut them up and stick toothpicks in them."

The thought of chicken tenders from the Tasty Chick made Laurie's mouth water. "Sounds like supper to me," she said grabbing her jacket. "Let's go."

The Tasty Chick across the street from St. Mark's was a small restaurant with a big impact in the community. There were only a few tables for patrons dining in, but the restaurant did a thriving carry-out business. They made the best fried chicken in the county and, as their sign proclaimed, the best chicken tenders this side of Eatonton. Laurie had finally stopped in Eatonton with Chase when they went to visit his family for Thanksgiving, and as both could attest, the Tasty Chick's chicken tenders beat Eatonton's hands down.

Chase paid for four orders of chicken tenders, and while he and Laurie waited at the counter she counted the cars across the street at St. Mark's parking lot. "Looks like the flower guild is there at least. I guess this is their show tonight."

Bessie, the woman at the counter, handed Chase a stack of square Styrofoam containers with red-checked waxed paper sticking out. The aroma was intoxicating. "Somebody's hungry tonight," she commented.

"Party across the street," Chase said. "Join us when you get off work."

"I just might do that!"

They drove to the church and entered the building through the kitchen where an assortment of snacks were already arrayed on the counter. "Glad we opted for tenders," Laurie said, pointing at the slices of cheddar, swiss, and pepper-jack arrayed next to a plate full of crackers.

Tracy, one of their choir friends, was making coffee and setting out sugar and creamer. "Hey, is that what I think it is?" she said, inhaling deeply as they came in. "Chase, honey. You can bring those tenders right here and leave them with me."

"I'll leave them with you, but don't make too many of them disappear before we're done working. Where is everybody?"

"A couple of guys are getting things down from the attic. The rest are in the nave."

They headed down the hall, and Chase was soon drafted to carry boxes of decorations.

Second Home

Laurie went on ahead to the nave where a small crew was already busy. Carol worked with several women getting the kinks out of lengths of artificial pine garland. "Fluff it up, girls. Make it look nice and full." She demonstrated as she talked.

Evelyn and Anne stood several pews away in front of a row of wreaths, trying to bring life back into crumpled red bows. Two larger lighted wreaths were propped up behind the altar where Don was setting up a ladder.

Laurie joined Carol and her crew working on the garland. "I hope Don's not planning to climb that ladder," she said. "Surely we can find someone younger to do it. Maybe I should ask Chase."

"Evelyn's brothers are here from Atlanta," Carol said. "I think they're still up in the attic handing down boxes, but they hung those wreaths behind the altar last year."

"If they're anything like Evelyn they should be perfect," Laurie said.

"What do you mean?" Carol looked at her blankly.

"They must be tall. Evelyn is ... what, five foot ten?" Laurie said.

Carol looked at Laurie with an indulgent smile. "Apparently you've never met Evelyn's brothers. They're built more like fireplugs than like Evelyn."

That's interesting, Laurie thought. Then again, it fit with her idea that Evelyn was the spoiled sister in a family of boys. She glanced at Evelyn and noted the cute boots she was wearing, and the stylish tunic draped over her leggings. "Do her brothers come here for every holiday?"

"No, but they do come fairly often," Carol said. "Their mother Nancy is in the memory care unit in that assisted living place up Redding Road. She can't travel anymore. And since their grandfather was the rector here—"

Laurie interrupted with an exclamation. "Really! I never knew that."

"Uh-huh. Tom Thigpen. His ashes are right out there with his wife Ruth's." Carol pointed through the window toward the columbarium. "This is the family's home church."

As Laurie fluffed garland, she watched everyone work. In the courtyard a few guys untangled light strings. Finally two stocky men entered the nave carrying another ladder. Chase followed behind them, and walked over to Laurie.

"Who are those two guys?" she asked him.

"Their names are Bob and Dave. Warren, I think." He pointed to each as he said their names.

"They're related to someone here. What are you doing?"

"I'm fluffing. See?" She untwisted and spread out branches of faux pine garland.

"Very fluffy. I always knew you'd make a great fluffer." He looked at the garland stretched out over three pews. "Looks like you have about two miles of it here. Where's it all going to go?"

Laurie pointed up along the woodwork that ran above the windows and all around the nave.

"Where's your friend Mary?" Chase suddenly asked. "I expected Pete to be here helping us."

"Mary texted me something about the babysitter couldn't keep Roly tonight and she and Pete decided to stay home. She needs that sitter on Christmas Eve, so I hope there isn't a problem."

"Chase. Grab an end of that and drag it over here." One of the guys, either Bob or Dave, pointed at the garland and set up his ladder at the back of the nave.

- "Break time is over," Chase said. He grabbed one end of garland and carefully pulled it along, handing it to the man on the ladder who hooked it on nearly-invisible nails spaced at intervals along the molding.

The fluffing crew had finished with the garland, .and went to help puff wreath ribbons. Others used lengths of red-velvet ribbon to hang wreaths from the ends of every other pew, while Evelyn affixed greenery around the baptismal font.

One of the brothers hung the two lighted wreaths on the wall behind the altar, and two Christmas trees covered in white lights miraculously appeared at either end of the communion rail. The whole place was starting to look like a holiday decorating scene in a magazine.

Joan dragged out a vacuum and swept up fake pine needles. Laurie joined Chase in the courtyard, watching as he helped a guy on a ladder hang white lights. It was brisk and cool outside. A concrete urn normally filled with seasonal flowers had been moved into the center of the courtyard and now held a Christmas tree-shaped rosemary bush. Laurie grabbed a branch of rosemary and crushed it to release the piney fragrance.

The man on the ladder descended and checked his handiwork, slapping the dust from his jacket. Then he offered his hand to Chase. "Looks like Miller time, buddy." He grabbed the ladder and carried it to his truck in the parking lot.

Laurie slipped her hand in Chase's and they admired the decorations. Through the windows the nave looked warm and festive. The red carpet that

ran up the center aisle and throughout the sanctuary
was a perfect shade to set off the greenery, and with
the soaring wooden ceiling, it reminded Laurie of a
lodge in the woods. All that was missing was a fireplace with a blazing yule log, and a moose head over
the altar. "Isn't it beautiful?"

"Wait until Christmas Eve. It'll be even nicer,"
Chase said. He gave her a quick kiss on the lips.

Laurie wrapped her arms around his waist, pulling him closer. "You're so nice and warm," she said,
burrowing her head into his shoulder. They held
each other as the sound of the vacuum cleaner
whirred and then switched off.

"Come on," Chase said. "Those chicken tenders
are calling."

He led her inside and into the kitchen. Snacks
were arrayed as on most Sunday mornings, except
now there were bottles of wine on the end of the
counter where pitchers of iced tea usually sat. People
loaded snacks onto plates and grabbed drinks to carry into the parish hall.

"Man, this place needs some music!" Chase pulled
his phone out of his pocket, and soon had it pumping
out jazzy holiday tunes. Laurie poured wine for herself and Chase into short plastic tumblers, and carried them into the parish hall where Barbara, Don,

and Joan were already in conversation. Laurie was about to go back into the kitchen for snacks when something Don said got her attention.

"Not long after the first of the year," Don was saying. "The kids will be in town between Christmas and New Year and can help me pack up what I'm keeping, and take what they want. Then whoever I get to run the estate sale can handle the rest. What doesn't sell I'll bring to the Treasure Chest. Hopefully I won't swamp you with *stuff*."

Chase entered and stood beside Laurie, his plate mounded with food. "Hey. Aren't you getting something to eat?"

She shushed him with a wave of her hand. "Don, I missed the first part of that," she said. "Are you moving?"

"I'm going to North Carolina to live near my son. I'll be renting a place in a senior citizens' neighborhood. Hopefully I'll like it real well and decide to stay put."

"I heard you say something about an estate sale." Laurie had never been to Don and Alice's house, but assumed it was a large one, and full of "stuff" as Don called it. Probably *nice* stuff, because Alice had good taste, and Laurie knew the couple hadn't ever lacked for funds.

Chase looked at Laurie, his eyebrows raised. Then he said to Don, "If we can do anything to help, let us know."

After visiting for a while Don left the parish hall. Barbara and Joan went back to the kitchen, leaving Laurie and Chase across the table from each other. As she nibbled the food on his plate, Laurie looked past him to where Evelyn and her brothers were engaged in lively conversation with Anne and her husband.

Laurie leaned closer to Chase. "If those boys are her brothers, then I'm her long-lost grandma. They look nothing alike! There's absolutely no family resemblance."

Chase started to turn. "No, no!" Laurie hissed. "Don't look."

He laughed as her face began to color, and gently took her hand. She shook her head at him. "Dirty rat," she said. "Are you almost ready to go? Tomorrow is a work day for some of us."

"Yes, just about." Chase stuck a fork in the last piece of chicken on his plate and popped it into his mouth.

As he chewed Laurie said, "I was a little surprised to hear Don is moving. But for a guy at his time of life, recently widowed, it makes sense that he would want to be closer to someone in his family. I'll have to keep my ears open for the date of that estate sale. Don't you imagine he and Alice had a lot of nice things?"

"I don't have to imagine. I know they did. I went to Don's house when he was having that problem with his heating system. I didn't see the whole place, but ..."

"Oh, yeah!" Laurie remembered. "So what was it like?"

"Classic furniture, fairly traditional, but not stuffy. Not your grandmother's traditional. And then some of the furniture, like in the den, was a little less formal. But who knows how much he and his kids will keep and how much he'll actually be selling."

"Guess we'll have to wait and see," Laurie said.

Chapter 14.

Two days before Christmas, Laurie paced around Chase's living room waiting for him to return from a quick run to the convenience store. Occasionally she glanced out the window, but between the early nightfall of winter and the bright light in the parking lot, the view was uninspiring.

A more interesting scene was visible through the little window in the oven door. They were baking cookies to serve on Christmas Eve when their friends came over for supper. The delicious smell filled the small apartment, and Laurie couldn't wait to bite the head off a gingerbread boy.

Despite the good smells and their holiday plans, there was still something missing.

Chase returned from the store and stashed the coffee creamer in the fridge. He hung his jacket and rubbed his cold hands together. "How are the cookies?"

"Two more minutes. Chase, I just wish we had some Christmas decorations." There was an uncharacteristic whine to Laurie's voice. She frowned at the small crèche sitting on the bookcase next to the couch. She had found it in the bottom of her box of winter clothes, the only decoration she had kept because it pre-dated her marriage to DB, and brought it to Chase's apartment.

Chase sighed. "I know. But where would we put more decorations? Like, where could we put a tree?"

"Maybe there." She pointed directly in front of the TV, a recent addition to his apartment.

Chase laughed. "Right there, huh?"

"Well, we don't watch it that much," she argued.

"True, we don't." He looked at her sad face. "Hey, we agreed not to spend a lot of money on things like that until we move to our house. Plus we're saving up for furniture, aren't we? Oh." He pulled her into his arms. "What, are you PMS-ing again?"

She pulled away, scowling. "It has nothing to do with my hormones!" This was Laurie's first Christmas in Georgia, and things just didn't feel right. She missed her family back home, familiar scenes, and familiar traditions. "I want my first Christmas in Georgia to be amazing, not plain and boring."

Chase looked at her pensively until the kitchen timer sounded. He slid the cookie sheet from the oven and placed it on a cooling rack. He lifted a cookie

with a spatula, waved it up and down, and blew on it
for a moment. Then he carried it to Laurie as a peace
offering.

Laurie blew on it a second more and then savagely
bit the gingerbread boy's head off with a growl. Her
eyes flew open with a look of amazement, and she
waved her free hand.

"Delicious, isn't it?" Chase said.

"Yeah, it is," she answered, clearly thinking of
something else. "I just had a fabulous idea! Why
didn't I think of this before? There's a Christmas
tree at the Treasure Chest!" She beamed.

"So?"

"So, we can go get it and set it up here!" Laurie
did not add "duh," but it was certainly implied by her
tone. "The shop is closed for the holidays. No one will
care if we borrow a few decorations." She gleefully
bit the arm off the gingerbread boy. "Oh, this is
good!"

Chase took the cookie from her and nibbled the
other arm. "But the tree's already set up in the
shop."

"Well, it's not that big. Couldn't we throw a trash
bag over it and haul it over here in the bed of your
truck, if you tie it down and drive slow?"

He made an *I'm-not-so-sure-about-this* face, bit a leg off the cookie, and watched as Laurie shoved his couch a couple of inches to make more room for the tree. There was a look of ecstatic determination on her face. He popped the rest of the cookie in his mouth. "Darling, how can I deny you anything? Let me just transfer these cookies to a plate and put the rest of the dough in the fridge."

Minutes later they crossed the railroad tracks and headed toward the Treasure Chest. "I'm sure we still have some Christmas tree skirts, and while we're at it we might as well get a Christmas-y table cloth. And a platter, and something for the cookies. And wouldn't it be nice to have some real champagne flutes? Except I don't remember seeing any of those at the shop."

Laurie rummaged in her purse and pulled out her key to the Treasure Chest. Chase stood close behind her and looked around. "There's no alarm on the building, is there?"

"Who's going to rob a charity thrift shop?" Laurie asked. "Don't answer that, come to think of it!" A robbery had occurred early in the summer.

"Exactly. So if I hear sirens, I don't know you and I'm running the other way."

"Hey. I'm one of the chosen ones. I have a key, remember? And it's your fault anyway because you gave me the idea. You were the one who wanted to sneak into 501 Evergreen Drive after dark." The bells on the door jangled as she pushed it open. She turned on some lights and headed down the hall to the Christmas room.

The tree stood right where it had been, looking a little bare due to the recent sale. Laurie plugged it in and tried to sound encouraging. "Look how cute it is."

"At least it already has the lights on it. It looks a little naked, though."

"Here. Start decorating." She grabbed a basket of ornaments labeled "25 cents each" and they added some to the tree.

Chase looked up, but continued decorating as headlights from a passing car cast shadows on the wall. "It definitely looks better now," he said. "And you think there's a tree skirt here somewhere?" He looked around on the tables, spotting a stuffed toy gorilla wearing a Santa Claus hat, and impulsively squeezed its paw. Laurie jumped as the silent shop suddenly vibrated with a throaty rendition of "Merry Christmas Baby."

"You idiot, you scared the crap out of me!" She slugged Chase on the arm.

"Wait, wait. I hear something," Chase said, standing still with his head up. "I think someone's here."

"Oh, stop! I have the heebie-jeebies as it is."

"No, seriously."

Laurie held her breath, looking around. "It sounded like the bells on the door," Chase whispered.

She tensed, and moved closer to him. Her shoulders relaxed when Mary appeared in the hallway. "I've heard of tree trimming parties, but I thought people had them in their *own* house, and not in the store."

"What are you doing here?" Laurie said.

"One might ask you the same question, girl-friend." Mary raised her eyebrows and gave her a smile. "I decided I had to come back for that shape-sorter truck toy thingy for Ricky, if it hasn't been sold. Pete's out in the car. I thought I recognized Chase's truck, but I told him if he didn't see me in three minutes he should call the cops. You know, you should have locked the shop door behind you. Any-one could wander in."

"I decided I couldn't have Christmas without a tree. It seemed a shame for this one to go to waste."

"I'll pretend to be surprised when we come over for dinner tomorrow," Mary said. "Meanwhile, I'm going to nab that toy and leave my I.O.U."

Mary disappeared up the hall, and Laurie turned to Chase. "Okay, before this party gets any wilder, let's throw the trash bag over this baby and get it out to the truck."

They bagged the tree, cinching it closed at the bottom. Then Chase dragged it to the door, and stepped out to ask Pete to give him a hand. Chase climbed up into the bed of the truck and pulled while Pete lifted from below. Together they got the tree loaded and secured.

Laurie came out a moment later with a cardboard box and shoved it into the truck next to the tree. "Did you get me the gorilla?" Chase asked.

"You'll have to wait until Christmas to find out, now, won't you?"

"You're a tease, Laura May," he smiled, kissing her by the light of the street lamp.

* * *

Laurie hit the snooze button on the alarm and pulled the covers over her head, but it was no use. She was wide awake. At least she'd remembered to set the alarm for later than usual. It was going to be a long day, ending with the "midnight" Christmas Eve service at St. Mark's, which actually started at ten p.m.

She pulled the covers off her head and listened. The shower wasn't running, but a smell of coffee wafted through the apartment. She put on her robe, stuck her cold feet into her slippers and padded into the deserted living room. A note on the kitchen counter said "back soon."

Laurie grabbed a travel mug out of the cupboard, filled it with coffee, and carried it to her apartment on the third floor. It sometimes seemed a waste of rent money, but she had enjoyed having a place of her own to escape to. She wouldn't for much longer, but now she was looking forward to setting up her pretty little boudoir.

Wait a minute, Laurie thought as her brain did a rewind. She and Chase had decided to keep both apartments until their leases were up. But when exactly would that be? She made a mental note to check. She showered, then checked her phone for messages, and saw one from Chase.

Breakfast in 30 minutes?

After a quick text back she finished her make-up and hair, and stared into her closet. So much winter clothing, and so little time to wear it all. She'd collected a lot of sweaters living up north. She selected a pretty blue and white Scandinavian-looking pullover to wear over her long sleeved jersey and jeans. Then she scampered back down to Chase's apartment.

Chase pulled a perfectly golden-brown waffle out of the waffle iron and added it to the small stack keeping warm in the oven. Laurie looked around, wondering where he'd been. She didn't see anything out of the ordinary on the breakfast table. Then she glanced at the stack of presents under the tree, which seemed bigger than she'd remembered, and smiled.

"That tree is looking better and better," she said.

"You think so? You're looking pretty good too." He turned businesslike as he placed the waffles on the table and added the toppings. "I figured we'd have a good breakfast this morning, and a light lunch before the early service, and then dinner with our friends before the late service."

They spent the day relaxing and taking it easy. Laurie stretched out on Chase's couch with her head propped on a pillow, reading an anthology of Southern writers while Chase listened to music and practiced on his old guitar.

Finally he got up, stretched and rolled his shoulders. "I've been sitting too long. We need to move around, get some exercise."

"I'm reading," Laurie mumbled.

Chase came and took a seat on the carpet beside the couch. He ran a fingernail along the bottom of her foot. Her leg twitched and she rubbed the sole of her foot against the couch cushion.

"Hey," he said. "Do you want to go for a walk or something?"

By way of answer Laurie read a line from the book aloud. "'The grandmother said she would tell them a story if they would keep quiet.'" She continued reading silently.

Chase ran his fingernail along the sole of her other foot. This time Laurie drew her knees up and slid her feet under the couch cushion.

In a soft voice Chase sang, "Itsy-bitsy spider went up the water spout," walking his fingers along her shin, over her knee and on up along Laurie's thigh.

"You know what we do to spiders don't you?" Laurie asked. With her teeth gritted she raised the book over her head and swung it down to swat him.

At the last minute he pulled his hand away and she smacked her thigh. "Ouch! You dirty rat!"

She set her book aside, rolled off the couch and straddled him, pinning his shoulders down on the carpet. "What are you gonna do now, huh? Huh?" she dared him with a devilish smile.

It was all the encouragement he needed. He reached his hands around her arms and found all the tender parts of her body. She squirmed, laughing, and tried to protect herself until somehow they had reversed places, and she was lying on the carpet beneath him, her hands pinned over her head. He looked softly into her eyes, then lowered his lips to hers and kissed her, tenderly at first, and then harder as she kissed back.

Chase released Laurie's hands, and continued kissing her cheek, her ear, her neck, while one hand explored under her sweater. She pulled him tighter and pressed against him, caressing his neck and shoulders. She slid her hands down to his waist and under his shirt, and then quickly spider-walked her fingers along his ribs.

Chase writhed and jerked up, looking down at her. "Who's the dirty rat now?" He grabbed her by the wrists, raising her hands above her head again, and thrust his hips against her, nibbling her neck.

She moved beneath him, and moaned softly. "Only one problem with you pinning my arms back," she said. "How are you going to get my clothes off?"

"Why would I want to do that?" he asked, his breath hot against her cheek as he continued kissing her.

"So we could ... do things."

"What things do you want to do?" he asked, running his tongue along the edge of her ear and pressing harder against her.

Laurie moaned again. "Things that would be more comfortable in the bed," she said.

He leaned back and smiled at her, scrambled onto his feet, and gave her a hand up from the floor. He put his arms around her, reached behind her, and pulled the sweater over her head. She wove her fingers into his hair, and kissed him again as he slid his hands under her shirt. "I'm enjoying doing things right here in the living room." He drew his warm hands along her rib cage, caressed her breasts, and grazed her earlobe with his teeth.

"We're going to get cold out here," Laurie said, struggling to unfasten his jeans. She finally got the button undone, and slid the zipper down, rubbing her hand over the tightly-stretched denim. "It'll be nice and cozy under the covers." She clutched the fabric over his hips and tugged.

"You win," he said. He grabbed her sweater off the floor, and they stumbled in each other's arms into the bedroom.

* * *

They made love and then slept, skin against skin in the warm bed, for the better part of an hour. Afterwards they ate lunch and Laurie went to her apartment to get cleaned up for the evening while Chase did some prep work on the dinner they would have between services.

Laurie fixed her make-up and put on a red sweater in soft cashmere over a gray wool skirt. She decided to wear her woolens while she could, and red was always a good color on her. The people at church would hardly see what she was wearing, but she wanted to look a little festive. She was tempted to put her hair in a French twist, but doubted the style would hold up well after she pulled her choir robe on and off a couple of times. She combed her hair smooth, fluffed up her bangs, and slipped on a pair of comfortable flats.

She met Chase in his apartment downstairs. "I haven't seen that sweater before," he said. He reached out to touch her shoulder, and began stroking her arms. "Ooh, soft. Maybe we need some more '*exercise.*"

"Don't start that, or we'll never get anywhere." Laurie pulled away, but gave his hand a squeeze. "Besides, we'll be tromping up and down the stairs to the choir loft. I'm sure we'll be exhausted by the time the late service is over." She glanced around the kitchen. The table was laid for four, and recently-acquired champagne glasses sat on the counter. "Something smells good in here."

Chase waved a hand toward the oven. "Rosemary chicken, carrots, celery, and potatoes, all in the roasting pan, slowly simmering in broth. It'll be fall-off-the-bone tender by the time the first service is done." He gave the temperature control a tweak. "Let's go."

Chapter 15.

It was twilight when Laurie and Chase arrived at St. Mark's. Soft light glowed through the windows of the church, and the courtyard outside was illuminated by strings of white lights. Extra lanterns had been placed strategically around the garden. Laurie noticed one that was placed where she knew Alice's ashes were buried.

Inside, a few new decorations had appeared since the greening of the church. A crèche now stood in front of the altar. The little manger was empty, awaiting the arrival of baby Jesus.

Light glinted on shiny brass up in the choir loft. Laurie looked up and saw Steve and several others. Suddenly the air came alive with a trumpet and the organ playing "Joy to the World."

She climbed the steps into the loft and took her seat next to Mary. "Looks like we're in for a treat," Laurie said.

"Yes. I can't believe Steve found a brass player who was available tonight. I don't know who this kid is, but evidently he's home in Chinkapin on college break. Lucky us."

"Thank you, that'll be fine," Steve said as the trumpeter blew his last note. "All right, choir, since most of us are here, let's get started. It shouldn't be as hard as singing first thing in the morning."

They reviewed the hymns and sang through the anthem, but cut their rehearsal short as the nave started to fill. Families crowded into pews. Ushers rushed to set up folding chairs in the aisle. Choir members robed and returned to the loft to lead the congregation in Christmas carols.

At last they assembled for the procession as candles on the altar were lit. "Angels from the Realms of Glory" sounded from the organ, and the procession started down the aisle. The verger, crucifer, and altar servers were joined by a child carrying the statue of the infant Jesus to place in the empty manger.

Laurie carefully wove her way along the aisle, trying not to bump anyone on a folding chair or knock a wreath off the end of a pew. She was glad to make it safely back to the loft.

There were readings from Isaiah and Titus, another carol, and the familiar Christmas story from Luke's gospel. Mother Barbara invited the children up for a special homily, and the children in turn treated the congregation to "Away in a Manger."

As the service came to a close, the altar servers and Mother Barbara processed down the aisle to a festive rendition of "Angels We Have Heard on High." Then the ushers turned the lights down low, and everyone sang along as Chase played "Silent Night" on his guitar. Laurie looked from the candles flickering on the altar to the wreaths at the front of the church and the lights sparkling outside in the courtyard. The church had never seemed more beautiful.

The congregation was enthralled. A hush hung over the nave as the final chord slowly faded. At last Mother Barbara said, "Merry Christmas everyone." As if they were suddenly given permission to move and speak, voices rose and people responded with their own Christmas wishes.

While Chase put away his guitar, Laurie went downstairs to mingle. There was no coffee hour, but a lot of visitors remained chatting. Anne was there with her three children and a couple of grandchildren, and Laurie wished her a Merry Christmas. "It's so nice to see so many people here. I wonder if anyone will even be coming to the late service."

"This is a good crowd, but you'll be surprised. The church will be full again later. I actually prefer the late service, but since the grandchildren are here we came early."

Laurie noticed Evelyn's brothers, Bob and Dave, chatting a few pews away. Again she was struck by the lack of family resemblance between the men and their sister. She knew Anne and Evelyn were good friends, so she hazarded a comment. "If I didn't know they were all siblings, I'd think someone was adopted," she said, gesturing toward the group.

Anne gave her a searching look, but said lightly, "Evelyn always says they got the muscles and she got the looks."

Laurie had a feeling she was touching on a delicate subject, and looked for a way to extricate herself. "Well, they sure were a big help decorating the church." She was relieved to find Mary at her elbow. "You about ready to come over for some supper? You're not stopping at home to check on Roly, are you?"

"Maybe later. I'm afraid if we go home now we'll just wake him up. See you at Chase's apartment in a few minutes."

"You'll love our beautiful decorations," Laurie said with a wink.

They made short work of the delicious roast chicken, and sat in the living room drinking champagne and eating gingerbread cookies while Mary admired the tree. "This looks better here than it did at the Treasure Chest. And I'm glad someone got this tree skirt. I thought it was so cute. To think you got all this for half price."

"Right? Who was it that used to say 'never pay retail'?" Laurie said.

"I don't know, but I'm stealing it for my Instagram. And look at all the pretty presents! Are you guys opening them as soon as you get home from the late service?"

"No," Chase said. "We are going to crash, sleep late, and open them tomorrow."

"While drinking coffee and eating cinnamon rolls," Laurie added.

"Such party animals," Pete said.

"Bet we get up earlier than you tomorrow," Mary said rolling her eyes. "I hope Ricky sleeps late, but it's not likely."

"Well, take some pictures of him 'unwrapping' presents. Hey, did you notice Evelyn and her family were at the early service? I still think she and those brothers must have had different parents. There's just no resemblance at all. But no one will say anything."

"The way families are blended together these days, maybe they're *not* related," Chase said.

Laurie ignored him. "I thought Anne would know for sure, but she was pretty tight-lipped."

"Yeah, but it's not like they've known each other since childhood, or anything," Mary said. "Didn't she and her husband move here from Louisiana or somewhere?"

Pete chimed in. "And did you know they found Mary under a cabbage leaf in Springfield, Ohio? Seriously guys, what does it matter?"

"Well, we have to rag on someone," Laurie said. "She's just our favorite person to be catty about."

"I thought I heard Mother Barbara say 'thou shalt not be catty on Christmas Eve,'" Pete said. "Isn't that right Chase?"

"Right. 'God bless us, everyone' and thou shalt not gossip, or something like that."

"We don't gossip," Laurie said defensively.

"You do too gossip! All the time. Why do you think I didn't tell you about Alice's illness, and the song Charlotte commissioned me to write? I knew you couldn't keep it to yourself."

"Well, what do you guys talk about, if not your friends and your family?" Mary asked.

"Golf," Pete said.

"Work. Fishing," Chase added. "You two should just admit you don't like Evelyn, and let it go."

"Easy for you to say," Laurie said. "You don't have to work with her." But she did feel a little guilty. She wanted to be the nice person Chase thought she was. She knew how tender-hearted he was, and she certainly didn't want him to regret asking her to marry him. She decided she'd better drop any more discussion about Evelyn, and changed the subject.

"Hey, I've been thinking. We still need to set a date for the wedding. How about right when our apartment leases are up? It's just a couple of months, but by that time we should have everything ready in the new house. We could get married, and then move right in."

Chase pulled his phone out of his pocket and looked at the calendar. "Hmmm. I think we could make it work. I wonder what the chances are of getting our deposits back."

"When would this be, again?" Mary asked. Chase tipped his phone toward her and tapped the screen. "Sweet," she said. "The weather should be pretty by then. Time for you two to get busy!"

* * *

A fog had descended on Chinkapin by the time the friends made their way slowly back to St. Mark's. There was a good crowd in the nave, as Anne had predicted. Choir members greeted each other as they pulled on their robes, and warmed up by leading the congregation in more Christmas carols.

The service was much the same as the early one. Mother Barbara offered a short sermon instead of a 'children's moment,' and a few of the hymns were changed. Laurie yawned as she hung up her choir robe after the service.

"I'm feeling the same way. I just hope you-know-who sleeps late tomorrow," Mary said.

"Merry Christmas, girlfriend. I'll see you when I see you," Laurie said, and gave her friend a hug.

* * *

Laurie woke to the sound of soft strumming on a guitar. She rolled onto her back and listened. The music was beautiful: gentle and peaceful. At first she thought it must be Chase, playing in the living room.

When a woman's voice started singing a Christmas song she hoped it was a recording.

Then the scent of coffee wafted into the room, and Laurie smiled. *It's a wonderful life*, she thought, slipping out of bed and pulling on her robe.

She found Chase in the kitchen. On the counter in front of him there was a rectangle of dough. Laurie put her arms around his waist, and watched over his shoulder as he smeared the dough with a cinnamon, sugar, and nuts concoction. "Merry Christmas to you, Merry Christmas to you, Merry Christmas dear Cha-ase." Then she gave him a kiss on the cheek.

"Merry Christmas to you," he said, and turned his head to kiss her on the lips. "I just have to roll this, slice it, mark it with a b, and put it in the oven for baby and me."

"It's gonna be good. But first, coffee, as the saying goes." She filled a mug, and padded into the living room to turn on the Christmas tree lights and admire the presents underneath it.

The oven door creaked open and shut, and Chase appeared in the living room with his mug. "Okay. Who goes first? You said your family didn't just fall upon the presents and tear them open willy-nilly, so I guess you want to do this in an orderly fashion."

"That's right."

First they opened presents from Laurie's family, including a new purse from her sister. There were no gifts from Chase's family, since they would be seeing them later in the week.

"Now you can open that one." Laurie pointed to the guitar Chase had picked out in the pawn shop, which leaned against the wall next to the tree.

He tore the red bow off the neck of the instrument and brushed his fingers across the strings a few times. Then he strummed as he sang, "We wish you a merry Christmas."

As Laurie applauded, Chase took a bow and blew her a thank-you kiss. "Now you can open this one." He handed her a rectangular box wrapped in red and gold.

She shook it but it didn't make any noise. Inside was a string of creamy white pearls on a bed of cotton, with a pair of pearl earrings nestled in the center. "Pretty! I like these."

"Those are the real deal, mind you, not beads. The finest the pawn shop had to offer."

"You must be one of their best customers," Laurie laughed.

"Well, I *was* shopping for you the night I found the guitar. You don't have much jewelry, but I know you like it. Mary told me you got rid of everything DB gave you."

"I did, what little there was. And now I can start over again. Thank you." She scrambled under the tree and pulled out a bulky rectangular package. "Now you have to open this one."

Laurie nervously shredded a bit of wrapping paper as Chase felt the edges of the package trying to imagine what was inside. "Too big for guitar strings. Guess I'm going to have to open it." He pulled the gift wrap off, along with a lot of protective paper, and stared, stunned, at the painting. "Where did you get this? You must have had it specially painted for me."

"It's kind of a long story," she said, remembering Jeff's attempted smooch under the mistletoe. "Someone from the arts center painted it." She watched his expression as an excited smile spread over his face.

"I *love* this! It's Beebee exactly. They must have used that old photo I have." His eyes roved over the painting. "And there's Beebee's squirrel!" Laurie nodded, feeling relieved. She was glad she'd spent the money on the painting, and not a new wedding dress that she'd probably only wear once.

"This is going to go somewhere special in our new house." He looked at her with eyebrows raised.

"Maybe in your music room, or somewhere."

Chase smiled and looked again at the painting. "We'll see."

"Are we done?" Laurie asked. "Those cinnamon rolls are smelling mighty good."

"One more." Chase handed her a small box covered in the same red and gold paper.

Laurie shook it, and something slid back and forth with a metallic clink. "Hmmm. More jewelry?" She shook it once more before tearing off the paper. Inside were a dozen tiny keys, some very plain and some decorative, all of which looked like they might unlock the box she had found in the house on Evergreen. "Cool. Where did you get all these?"

"Here and there." Chase smiled and shrugged. "I thought you'd have fun trying them out."

"It feels like having a dozen lottery tickets," Laurie said. "Maybe one of them will work."

Chapter 16.

Mary had warned Laurie how quickly Christmas would disappear from the Georgia landscape. Nevertheless, Laurie was surprised to see people taking their trees down, packing away the snowmen, Grinches, and deer from their front lawns, and basically cleaning up from the holiday immediately after the twenty-fifth. "You gotta remember," Mary said, "they've had all these decorations up since Thanksgiving. They're ready to move on. Most people around here don't give a hoot about Epiphany."

Laurie and the rest of the Treasure Chest volunteers got a text from Carol about a workday before New Years to pack away the leftover Christmas items and get the shop ready to re-open. Carol promised it wouldn't take long, and when Scott told Laurie she could leave after just a couple of hours at the *Journal*, she headed over to the thrift shop to help out.

Half a dozen workers scurried around the shop as Evelyn and Anne cleared the last of the Christmas items out of what was called the eclectic room ten months out of the year. Laurie walked in to have a look around. "Not much left to pack up, is there," she commented.

"I don't know who bought the Christmas tree that was in here," Anne said. "They must have come in the last day we were open. I know it was still in here Friday morning. Who worked that Saturday?"

"I did," Evelyn said. "And you and Virginia were there." She pointed at Laurie. "But I don't remember selling the tree."

"After you left, a young couple came in here and bought a bunch of Christmas stuff. They needed it in a hurry, and I knew we wanted to get rid of every-thing." Laurie wasn't lying. It *was* after Evelyn left. Several days after, in fact. And no one had to know that she and Chase were the young couple. She had grown fond of the little tree, so right after Christmas Laurie had let herself into the shop and left a vague note in the cash drawer, along with payment for the items.

Laurie escaped to the staff kitchen before Evelyn and Anne could ask any more questions. She found an old CD of mariachi music and put it in the little boom box. The shop came to life with the sound of a Mexican trumpet and a wild "Ah-hah-hah-hah" from the speaker, accompanied by the sound of the vacuum and the scratch of the broom.

Carol, Mary, and Laurie tackled one of the work rooms. It was chock full of non-clothing items which needed to be priced and put out for sale. There were pieces of mismatched china, glassware, and silverware, pot lids, odd linens, toys, vases, paintings, and home décor, and even some Christmas items that would just have to be stored until next year. A few things looked like they could be valuable collectables, if someone had the time to research them. Unopened bags and boxes held recent donations that no one had even had time to look into yet.

"This looks like office supplies," Mary said, digging down into a cardboard box that had been hidden under a set of bed sheets. "Do we want to keep any of this stuff to use here?"

Carol looked inside. "We can sure use these." She pulled an unopened packet of index cards out of the box.

"Check out this paperweight." Mary held up a crystal orb. "You wouldn't want to drop this on your foot."

Laurie glanced over. "Oh, I know where that came from. All that stuff was in Mother Barbara's office."

Mary pulled out a photo album. "This looks like its empty," she said, turning the pages. "What do you think? A dollar? Oh, wait. There are a few pictures in the back."

The others looked up. "Anything interesting?" Laurie asked.

"From the rector's office? Hah!" Carol said. "Probably something really exciting, like photos from a vestry retreat." She looked over Mary's shoulder. "Now that man is Rev. Thigpen. His picture is in the church office. He was three or four rectors ago, but he was here forever. Over twenty years, anyhow. He sure looks young in these pictures." She turned a page. "This is him again a few years on, with his wife Ruth, and that's their daughter Nancy. She's Evelyn's mother. She married a Warren. Now this here..." She tapped the page and looked up at the others. "This baby must be Evelyn, but good Lord, will you look at this bonnet."

Mary smiled. "I guess they wanted to see that baby coming. The bonnet looks like it would glow in the dark."

Laurie came around to look at the album. The old photo had faded, but she could tell the ribbons on the bonnet were bright hot shades of yellow, orange, and green.

"These boys are her brothers, Bob and Dave," Carol said, pointing to another picture. "They're twins, but you wouldn't know it, because they're not identical."

"I met those guys over Christmas," Laurie said. "I didn't realize they were twins."

"They were in my class at school," Carol said. "I guess that's their father, Mr. Warren. I don't remember him, because he died when they were in second grade or thereabouts." She clicked her tongue and shook her head. "Those kids practically grew up here at the church. Especially Evelyn. Let me show this to her. I'm sure she'll want to have these."

Laurie wondered what Carol meant, about the kids growing up at the church, but didn't have a chance to ask.

"I heard my name. Did you find something interesting?" Evelyn paused outside the work room carrying the few items of Christmas clothing to be saved for next year. "I need a storage bin for these."

"Look here at these pictures." Carol held up the album open to the picture of baby Evelyn with her mother and grandparents.

Evelyn's face lit. "Oh! Where did these come from? Are there more pictures?"

"Just a few right here," Carol said. "It came out of the church office."

Evelyn shifted her load of clothes and turned a page in the album. There was another photo of her mother and father with the two boys as toddlers. In the picture her mother was clearly pregnant. She turned back to the photo of herself in her mother's arms. "That must have been the only bonnet I owned. I think I came home from the hospital in it. I wish I knew whatever happened to it."

Evelyn thanked Carol, and walked back toward the office with the album under her arm.

* * *

The volunteers worked for most of an hour, putting price stickers or hang tags on items. As quickly as Anne and Evelyn got the few remaining Christmas items boxed up, others filled the eclectic room with picture frames, figurines, clocks, pottery, and anything else that had no other place at the Treasure Chest. A few items wound up out in the dumpster, with good reason, and more than a few ended up on the fifty-cent table outside the front door.

Finally Carol gathered everyone together. "Ladies, it's twelve o'clock. Do we want to break for lunch and have our meeting?"

They all agreed to call it quits. Anne walked through the shop turning off lights. Mary offered to drive over to the Tasty Chick, and took everyone's order. The rest trooped over to the parish hall while Laurie rode with Mary to help carry the food.

Laurie pulled open the door to the restaurant and the smell of fried chicken wafted out. It smelled almost as good as the scent of freshly ground coffee. As they stepped up to the counter to place their order, she recognized the woman who had waited on her and Chase the night of the greening of the church.

"Hi, Bessie. How are you today?"

"I'm doing great! Beloved and blessed, as Pastor Harden says."

"Beloved and blessed. I'm glad to hear that." Laurie smiled. "I guess we all are."

"Y'all having another party over at the church?" Bessie asked.

"A work day at the Treasure Chest," Mary said. "Time to box up the things left over from Christmas and get the place ready to re-open."

"I'll give y'all some extra napkins," Bessie said. She packed their order into a couple of large paper sacks. "Y'all have some really good sales. I found some nice shirts that I gave my son for Christmas, new ones with the tags still on. You need to let me know when you're having another sale."

Laurie promised to stop in and let her know. She noted how quick and efficient the woman was. The whole restaurant was run like a well-oiled machine. "Bessie, how long have you worked here?"

"Lord," she said with a laugh. She gazed through the window and then focused on Laurie again. "Has it been thirty years? More than that. Some days my feet say it's been forty!"

The gears in Laurie's mind clicked into place and she had a sudden idea to write a feature story about the Tasty Chick. After all, wasn't it an institution in Chinkapin? How did it get started, and how long had it been there? As long as the church, or longer? She mentioned it to Bessie, and said she'd get back to her.

"Come on," Mary said. "Everyone's waiting." She grabbed a sack and Laurie picked up the other.

"Come back," Bessie said with a nod.

Laurie placed one bag next to her feet and held the other in her lap as Mary drove across the street. "It took me a while to figure out that when people here say 'come back' they don't mean literally 'come back right this moment.' Like, when they say 'hey' they don't mean 'hey, I want to tell you something right now.'"

"Yep. One of those local things, I guess."

A few minutes later Laurie and Mary handed out the food orders. Someone had found a jug of iced tea in the refrigerator. Mother Barbara brought her lunch bag and joined the volunteers.

"How's everything at the Treasure Chest? Looking like Christmas never happened?"

"Just about," Carol said. "A few little items are out on the fifty-cent table, but everything else is packed and put away. We're ready to open again this weekend."

"I hate to remind you, but we'll have to take all the greenery and decorations down from the church in a week and a half. After the three wise men come at Epiphany that'll be it."

"It looks so good, though," Laurie said. "Really woodsy and all."

"Yes, but to everything there is a season, and a time for every purpose under heaven," Barbara quoted.

"I saw some trees out on the curb already," Mary said. "They always look so abandoned to me."

"You don't see so much of that anymore, since most people have artificial trees," Anne said.

"Okay, ladies, let's get the business done so we can all go home and collapse." Carol pulled a steno pad out of her purse, and rummaged for her reading glasses which she perched on the end of her nose. "I just want you to mark a few dates on your calendars. I was thinking about when to put the winter clothes on sale. What do you think about everything half price in February?"

"But not purses and shoes and lingerie," Evelyn said. "I mean, the bras are already just two dollars."

"Right," Carol agreed.

"Maybe we should put the coats and jackets on sale sooner," Mary suggested.

"I think we should put the coats and jackets at half price starting this week," Joan said. She folded her arms and looked at Evelyn.

"Why don't we just shovel everything out to the fifty-cent table?" Evelyn said hotly.

Joan didn't quail. "I'm not saying we should give the stuff away, but you know it starts to warm up here around the end of January. We still have a lot more winter clothing to put out. I was looking in the back room. We don't want to have to save those winter things until next year." She looked around the table for support.

Laurie agreed with Joan, and suspected several of the others did too. She waited to see if anyone would speak up.

Anne wrapped up her lunch papers and addressed Mary. "We don't want to have to pack up the coats and jackets and send them to Appalachia, either. For one thing it would take too many boxes." She turned to Carol. "How about half price on coats and jackets starting in the middle of January. If we have any more of those, we need to hurry and get them out."

Carol nodded. "I think that's a good idea. So if everyone agrees," she looked at Evelyn, "we'll have coats, jackets, and maybe the boots half-price starting the middle of the month. Let's see." She looked through her reading glasses to consult her calendar, and jotted a note on her steno pad. "And maybe we'll wait until the middle of February to make the rest of the clothes half price." Evelyn looked down her nose at Joan and took a sip of her tea.

Carol continued. "Then the first week in March they can be a dollar a piece, and after a couple of weeks we'll run our bag sale. At the end of March we'll have another work day and bring out the spring clothes. Does that sound all right?"

She looked around the table, but there was no more discussion. The volunteers all looked tired. Joan still sat with her arms folded. Mary stood and started gathering everyone's trash. Laurie just wanted to go home and find out what Chase was up to.

Mother Barbara offered to pray for the group. "The Lord be with you," she said.

"And also with you," they answered.

"O God, mercifully grant that your Holy Spirit may in all things direct and rule our hearts; that we may always remember it is your work we are called to do, and that all we think, do, or say may be pleasing in your sight. Amen."

Everyone said "Amen," and then left singly or in pairs. Laurie started to walk out with Mary, but Carol stopped her. "Laurie, would you be sure to put the sales up on Facebook so our customers have a heads up?"

"Sure, I'll be glad to." She pulled the bedraggled little notebook out of her purse. "Let me make sure I've got the right dates, since the discussion went back and forth."

By the time Laurie stuffed her notebook back in her bag, Mary had gone on her way, and Carol, Laurie, and Mother Barbara were the only ones left in the parish hall. "What is up with Evelyn?" Laurie asked Carol. "You're the volunteer committee chair, so why does Evelyn think she gets to call the shots all the time? Doesn't she realize we're all volunteers? I mean, shouldn't all of us get a say in when we have sales and things? We put stuff out for sale, and she carries it back to the back room. We price something one way, and she comes in and changes the price. We tag clothes, and before they get out on the sales floor she puts them in the mission box. And it's not just the Treasure Chest, it's here at the church too. It's like she owns the place, and everything will come crashing down if she doesn't keep it all going just the way she wants to. Why does she even care so much?"

"You're right," Carol agreed. "She doesn't own the place, but she did pretty much grow up here."

Laurie narrowed her eyes. "That's what you said over at the shop. So what was the deal?"

"Well, you know Reverend Thigpen was her grandfather." Laurie nodded and Carol continued. "And Evelyn's mother, Nancy, was a school teacher. She quit teaching after she got married and had the twins, and a couple years later Evelyn came along, like God's gift to the world. But then Nancy's husband died real young, so she went back to teaching in order to support her family. The boys were in school by then, and Evelyn was in kindergarten, but when they weren't in school, a lot of the time they were here at the church. Their grandmother Ruth worked in the church office. We didn't have a secretary, even part-time, in those days, and Evelyn, once she got a little older, used to help out folding bulletins and doing little jobs. She just had the run of the place."

"I could use some helpers like that," Mother Barbara said.

"For all intents and purposes Evelyn was a PK, a preacher's kid. She was a little angel when she was around the grown-ups, but she used to boss around all the other kids at church. That's where she gets some of her bossiness. And then she saw her mother being in charge in front of the classroom at school, and figured she should be in charge of all the kids there too."

"Some of us don't need another boss, and don't want to be told what to do. I wish there was a nice way to ask Evelyn to just..." Laurie had a few ideas, but didn't think it would be polite to say them out loud.

Carol shrugged. "She was one spoiled child."

Chapter 17.

January got off to a slow start at the *Journal,* and in Chinkapin in general. A romantic comedy was in the works at the Little Theater, which Laurie thought might be good for a couple of articles in a month or so. And February would see the fifth annual "Champagne and Chocolate" event at the Chinkapin Arts Center. Kids were back at school, and everyone was back at work, but there wasn't much in the newspaper.

Scott was working on a few items for the M. L. King holiday, but with no other news to report it was easy for Laurie to sell her feature ideas. He was enthusiastic about an article on the history of the Tasty Chick restaurant. It had been in business for years, and was still one of the most popular eateries in Chinkapin, even after all the fast food places had opened along the interstate just west of downtown.

She phoned the restaurant and Bessie picked up on the second ring. "Tasty Chick. How may I help you?" She sounded businesslike.

"Bessie, this is Laurie Lanton. I spoke to you the other day about writing an article about the Tasty Chick for the *Journal*."

"Yes! How are you today Ms. Laurie?" She sounded excited now, and actually giggled.

Laurie asked when would be a good time for an interview. She didn't want to interfere with Bessie's workday.

"We open at eleven o'clock, but I'm always at the restaurant by nine in the morning. If you want to come see me around then I could talk to you, show you how we prepare all the chicken, the coleslaw, the potatoes, all of that."

"That would be perfect," Laurie said. They agreed on the date, and Laurie hung up the phone and jotted down a few questions to prepare for the interview.

She had just finished when an event notice popped into her inbox: an announcement for an estate sale. She didn't even have to look up the address. It was Don and Alice's house.

This is sooner than I expected, she thought. Actually, the timing couldn't be better. It coincided nicely with another event on her calendar, one that wasn't in the newspaper. In about an hour she and Chase would be closing on the house on Evergreen Drive.

Second Home

***

Marshall & Copely was the law firm where Carol worked, and it happened to be right around the corner from the Coffee Pot. Laurie had a few minutes to kill, so she parked near the café and went in to grab a cappuccino before her appointment. She was at the counter gazing up at the menu board when the door opened behind her.

"Chase!" she said, and put her arm around his waist. "You found me."

"You're easy to find. All I have to do is follow the scent of coffee. And I saw you go in while I was parking the truck." He checked the time on his phone. "We might have time for a snack. I'm starved."

They ordered and sat on the old church pew at a table next to the wall. "An interesting event came to my attention this morning." Laurie looked at Chase with her eyebrows raised. "Don is holding an estate sale at the end of the week."

"Already! Sounds like good timing for us. I take it you want to go."

"Well, I keep thinking about that beautiful but mostly empty house we're going to take possession of today. It wouldn't hurt to get some used furniture, maybe not to keep forever, but just so our new house doesn't stay empty too long. Plus I would just like to see his place. You know I like to look at houses."

They ate their lunch and hurried over to the lawyer's office and into the small waiting area. Chase picked up a magazine and sat in a wing chair while Laurie spoke to the receptionist. "Hi. I'm Laurie Lanton and this is Chase Harris. We're here to see Mr. Marshall. Also, is Carol working today?"

"She is. She told me she had some friends from church coming in. I'll let them know y'all are here." She made a couple of calls on the intercom.

Laurie took a seat next to Chase. A moment later the door to the inner offices opened and they rose to greet a tall, cheerful man in a suit. "Laurie and Chase," he boomed, extending his hand to both in turn. "Good afternoon. I'm Greg Marshall. How are you today? Ready to get started?" They followed him past a few office doors into a conference room where a secretary was setting out stacks of paper. She offered coffee or water, but the two declined.

They took their seats as Carol leaned into the room. "Hey Laurie. Hey Chase. Are you all excited?"

"Yes, we're excited." Laurie smiled at Chase, who grabbed her hand under the table and squeezed.

"This is the fun part of my job," Greg said. "Clients are either excited to be buying a place or excited to be selling one. Either way, I enjoy this a lot more than wills and probate.

"As you know we're doing all the signing by fax, or whatever they call it these days. The sellers are standing by in Chicago, so this shouldn't take too long, especially since they're anxious to get it over with and go to lunch. I always try to take advantage of the time difference." Greg winked at Laurie. "Your realtor is on his way. He called just before you arrived. He's got some good news, but I'll let him share it."

Then he added to Laurie, "You're getting pretty famous around town. I see your byline in the *Journal* all the time, and I enjoy your articles."

"Thank you," Laurie said.

"I feel like I should ask for your autograph or something, but after today," he gestured toward the stack of papers in front of him, "you won't want to sign nothin' for a while!"

The realtor, Chad Houser, skidded into the room and took a seat across from Chase. "Sorry I'm late, folks. I have a new grandbaby! Arrived this morning. Her name is Hadley, but don't ask me all the pounds and inches and all that. All I know is she's healthy and my daughter's fine. Whoo! It was a long night, though."

"Congratulations," Laurie said. "Your first grand-child?"

"We have three grandsons, but this is the first girl. My wife is so excited. She's wanted a little granddaughter to dress up and have tea parties with. The boys just don't hold still for that."

Laurie thought for a moment about spoiled little girls, but was brought back to the business at hand by Greg's sonorous voice as he took up the first set of papers. Laurie and Chase both grabbed pens, and listened carefully to all the explanations, signing documents as they were passed along. Chad offered a few comments, but it was all straightforward.

Finally they'd signed the last of the papers, and the lawyer handed them a folder bulging with their copies. "Five-O-One Evergreen Drive is now yours. Well, yours and the bank's." He smiled. "So Mr. Houser, I presume you have some keys for them?"

They turned toward Chad, who suddenly looked queasy. He patted his pockets, and shook his portfolio, but there was no jingling of keys. "I seem to have left the keys at my office, with all the excitement this morning."

"No worries," Chase said. "I'll follow you to your office and pick them up. I don't think we wanted to go to the house this afternoon. Did we?" He looked at Laurie.

She shrugged. "Later will be fine."

* * *

Laurie didn't want to go to the empty house on Evergreen, but she didn't want to go to her apartment either. Instead she drove to the Treasure Chest, and when she saw Mary's car there she parked in the lot.

"Hey! How'd everything go?" Mary asked as soon as Laurie walked into the shop. Then she frowned. "I thought you would look happier. Did something go wrong at the closing?"

"Everything's fine. I now own a house that I don't have any keys to, but there's no furniture or anything in it, so..." She explained about Chad forgetting the keys, and the realtor's new grandbaby.

"I hope you told Chad about the Treasure Chest. We have all kinds of nice baby stuff."

"Dang. I missed that opportunity. Some publicity manager I am." Laurie craned her neck to look at the shelf in the hallway. "Isn't that display pretty. When did all the blue and white come in?" There was a lovely arrangement of blue and white porcelain plates, bowls, a ginger jar, and four teapots of varying sizes assembled on a pale blue cloth.

"Some of the pieces we've had, and a few came in earlier in the week. Anne and Evelyn worked on the display this morning."

Laurie raised her eyebrows. "Well, whoever did it, it looks nice. Before I forget, I'll post a picture on Facebook. I know some people who collect that stuff." She rummaged in her purse for her phone and snapped the photo. "Anyway, speaking of my empty- and waiting-to-be-decorated house, have you heard about the estate sale at Don's this weekend?" Laurie filled her in on all the details.

"I can't go Saturday," Mary said. "My sitter, Melissa, is having a birthday party for her oldest, and I promised I'd help."

"I'd like to run out there Friday, if I can convince Chase to escape from work and go with me. We at least need a couch, and a table to sit and eat at. Which reminds me, come help me carry some stuff in. Chase and I have been cleaning out closets, and I brought some clothes and what-nots to donate."

The two went out to Laurie's car and returned with several bags filled with clothes, shoes, and purses. Laurie pulled a purse out of the top of one bag. "I wasn't sure whether to hold on to this or get rid of it, but my sister sent me a new one for Christmas that I really love, and I can only carry one at a time."

Mary pulled a few shirts out of the bag and rummaged for some price tags.

"Now I *have* to do some shopping, or I'll be running naked through the streets. Where'd you get that cute top?" Laurie pointed to Mary's long-sleeved jersey. It was a pale shade of turquoise with ruffles down the front.

"Georgia Thriftique. They still have a few nice gowns there. You need to be thinking about a wedding dress, girl."

Laurie breathed a sigh. "Tell me something I *don't* know. I've got a lot to get done if Chase and I are going to get married in March. A couple of days ago we were discussing food for the wedding again. He's serious about putting on a big barbecue buffet. I'm just afraid my pretty little wedding will turn into some ... some shindig, hoedown, *hootenanny.*"

"Put your foot down. Don't let him push you around. It's your wedding too." Mary stopped and looked at Laurie. "Is that what I'm supposed to say?"

"Yeah, that's what you're supposed to say. You're supposed to be on my side."

"Okay, just checking. I know you get tired of me and my unsolicited advice. I really don't care what you serve at your wedding. If I don't like it I can always run to the Waffle House afterwards. It's you and Chase who have to agree."

"We do need to work it out." Laurie sighed again. "Part of me wants to stand up for what I want, and part of me really doesn't care either. It's just a party. And it's Chase's as much as mine."

"You could always elope," Mary suggested. "They say Gatlinburg is nice in the spring." Suddenly her face brightened. "Or, you could go out to Vegas and get married by Elvis!"

"Don't tempt me." Then she whispered to Mary, "Here comes the boss. Try to look busy."

Evelyn had been walking back and forth, pricing and setting out Valentine's Day items. There were figurines, stuffed toys, and wine glasses with hearts painted on them. There was even some lacy lingerie. Laurie made a mental note to look it over later, in case there was something lovely that she might want for her wedding night.

Evelyn handed Laurie a cardboard box containing half a dozen coffee mugs with various valentine's sentiments or pink and red hearts on them. "Put fifty-cent stickers on these, please, and let's get them out. If they don't go in the next month or so, we'll put them on the ten-cent table."

"Sure thing," Laurie said. She fetched a sheet of stickers from the office and stuck blue dots inside the mugs.

The bells on the door jangled as two older women entered the shop. "Hi, Alma," Mary said addressing the first. "I haven't seen you in a while. How are you doing today?"

"I'm doing great. Mary, this is my sister LuAnne. She's visiting from Waycross. I'm taking her to see all the exciting sites and scenes of Chinkapin. And tonight we're going to have dinner at the Salty Dog."

"Yum. I know you'll enjoy that. We've put out a lot of new stuff since Christmas, so have a look around."

"We will," LuAnne said, "but first I want to ask if you have any yarn."

"We usually do," Mary said a little uncertainly. "If we do it would be in the hall back near the linens room."

"We do have yarn," Evelyn confirmed as she walked back to the counter. She handed a couple of vases to Laurie and said, "Put a dollar on these." Then she asked LuAnne, "Are you looking for anything special?"

"Mostly what I need is number four acrylic yarn. I love to crochet," LuAnne explained.

"Somehow I didn't get the crochet gene," Alma said behind her hand to Mary.

"It's for Project Linus. Do you remember Linus from the Peanuts comic strip, how he always carried his security blanket everywhere he went?"

"Oh, yes, I remember," Evelyn said with a smile.

"Well, Project Linus makes blankets for children in need. The group I'm a part of gives out blankets at the hospital. You should see those kids' eyes just light up when we tell them they can pick out any blanket they want."

"I did make one blanket once," Alma said. "Remember? It was made out of scraps, all kinds of crazy colors, and I thought it was so ugly I didn't even want to give it to LuAnne, but she took it anyway, and do you know, one little boy went straight for that blanket, and wouldn't even look at the others. It made my day when Lu told me."

"I'll tell you what'll break your heart," LuAnne said. "I made a tiny little crib blanket out of white yarn. It was actually too small. But there was one young couple at the hospital whose baby was still-born. The daddy had seen us when we were setting up. He took that white blanket to wrap their poor little baby in, and they buried her in her coffin wrapped in that blanket. It just about makes my heart burst every time I think about it."

Tears welled up in Laurie's eyes as she listened to the story.

"Tell them about the girl who gave her baby up for adoption," Alma said.

"Oh, that's right. There was this young girl. She wasn't but fifteen when she got pregnant. And the daddy was one of the teachers at the high school. He lost his job over it. It was just awful!" LuAnne paused to blink at her sister. "But anyway, she delivered the baby and took one of our blankets for him, for the couple of days she was with him in the hospital. But then the people who adopted him mailed her the blanket back as a keepsake. Well, that girl's mother sent a thank-you card to our Linus chapter, and said that her daughter slept with that blanket in her bed, and it helped her get over, you know, having to give her baby up."

Evelyn had listened intently as LuAnne told her story. Then she said, "We just had a couple of boxes of yarn donated to us. I've been tripping over them all morning. The yarn hasn't even been put out for sale yet. If you'll follow me to the back, you can look through it and take what you want for your group to make blankets with."

Laurie raised her eyebrows and looked at Mary as Evelyn led the two sisters to the back of the shop. "Did she say 'take,'" Laurie said, "as in, for free?"

Mary put a finger up to her ear and pretended to clean it out. "That's what I thought I heard, but I can't believe it."

Laurie tagged the two vases and put them out for sale while Mary rang up another customer. She could hear talking and rummaging going on, and looked around the corner to see Evelyn and the two women pulling skeins of yarn out of a cardboard box, examining the labels, and packing them into another box.

"Wow, there *is* a lot of yarn back there," Laurie commented to Mary.

Finally the three women came back to the counter with two cardboard boxes full of yarn. "Write up ten dollars, would you?" Evelyn said to Laurie. "I'm going to price some more valentine items. You all make sure to look around the shop, now. We've got lots of nice new items."

"Did she say ten dollars?" Laurie whispered to Mary. She looked over the edge of the counter at the boxes. "That must be thirty skeins there, never used. And we usually charge a dollar a piece."

"Don't ask questions," Mary murmured.

The sisters shopped for a while, and purchased a couple of other items. Then Alma opened the door for them as Laurie picked up one box and LuAnne hoisted the other. "It was so good to meet you ladies," she said. "Alma talks about you all the time. And our Linus group is going to go wild when they see all the yarn I'm bringing back. Your little shop here will make a mighty big difference."

"So glad you stopped to see us," Mary said. "Safe travels. And Alma, come see us again soon."

Evelyn watched through the door as the women loaded the boxes into the trunk of the car. Then she pulled the "closed" sign down. "It's close enough to four o'clock," she said. "I don't know about you two, but I'm ready to call it a day."

"I'll go switch off some lights," Laurie said, leaving Evelyn and Mary to total up sales.

A few minutes later Laurie and Mary left the shop and stood chatting in the parking lot. As Evelyn's car pulled away Mary said, "We had a good day today, in spite of the deep discounts Evelyn gave on yarn." She smiled.

"I wonder what's gotten into her. That's the second time I've noticed her go crazy like that. Remember I told you about that pregnant girl who was in here with her mother?"

"Yeah. They've been back since then to buy some other stuff."

Laurie thought a minute. "That sure was a lot of yarn those women bought. How many blankets do you suppose they'll make with all that?"

"I don't know. A dozen? More? They'll make a lot of people happy."

Chapter 18.

A few days later, Laurie spent an hour at the *Journal* office getting her thoughts in order, and then drove to the Tasty Chick. Bessie unlocked the door to let her in.

"Thanks for taking time out of your morning to talk to me," Laurie said as Bessie brought her a cup of coffee.

"As a matter of fact we've been here since seven o'clock this morning. My fryer stopped working last night, but luckily I have a son who knows how to get things done." Bessie led Laurie back behind the counter. A man somewhat older than Laurie was tinkering with the fryer. It was pulled away from the wall to expose a tangle of electrical wires. "This is my son Anthony."

"Nice to meet you. That looks pretty serious back there."

"It's all over but the shoutin'. It needed a new thermostat, and I'm fixing to put everything back together now so Mama can get the oil heated up."

"That fryer is the heart of the restaurant," Bessie said. "If it's not working just right, nothing else matters."

"Anthony, are you an electrician then?" Laurie asked.

"Yes, Ma'am. I am on the maintenance crew at the chicken plant down in Hendricks. I do a little bit of this and that. Plumbing, electric, all like that."

"He works the night shift," Bessie said, steering Laurie back into the small dining area. "Now, what can I tell you about the Tasty Chick? What was it you wanted to ask me?" The way she said 'ask' sounded more like 'axe' to Laurie's ears.

"I'd love to hear the whole story. Whose idea was it to open a restaurant, and how did you wind up here in Chinkapin?"

"It was all up to my husband Oliver," Bessie began. "And he owed everything he knew about cooking to his Grandmother Avis and the U.S. Army."

She told the long, meandering story, and Laurie left the restaurant with pages and pages of notes. Back at her desk at the *Journal*, she tried to put it all in order.

Bessie's husband Oliver was a native of Chinkapin. He was drafted into the army during the Vietnam era, and served two tours as a cook. When he got out of the service he landed a job at Fort Benning as a chef in the officer's club. "We met on the army post," Bessie told her. "I was working in the commissary bakery. I know a thing or two about cooking myself. Well, we got married, and had two girls and then Anthony came along. He's the only one still living here; the girls both live in Alabama."

When Oliver's father died, the two packed up their family and moved to Chinkapin to live near his mother. At first Oliver worked in another restaurant on Redding Road. Then the place across from the church came up for sale, and the two were able to buy it with their savings and help from Oliver's mother.

Oliver was determined to make the business a success, and with Bessie by his side he did. All of their children worked in the restaurant at one time or another, and Bessie joined him full time when the kids no longer needed her at home.

The chicken batter recipe was a secret from Oliver's Grandmother Avis. The coleslaw was also her recipe, but Laurie managed to wheedle it out of Bessie so she could publish it in the paper. Oliver had learned to make French fries in the army. A few other menu items had changed over the years, but the basics stayed the same.

The Tasty Chick was now run by Bessie and four kitchen helpers, all of whom had worked in the restaurant for over twenty years. When Laurie asked what had become of Oliver, Bessie remained silent a moment shaking her head. Then finally she explained that Oliver had Parkinson's disease. It had come on slowly, forcing him to gradually throttle back his work at the restaurant. Now he spent his days trying to convince the VA that it must have been exposure to Agent Orange that caused his illness.

"He is going to be so excited when this article comes out in the paper. After his kids, the thing he's most proud of is this restaurant. He's going to be just so pleased. The *Journal* better print a whole lot extra, because we're going to buy fifty copies and send them to all the family."

Laurie finally saved her work and stepped into Scott's office. "Hey, I'm almost done with that article on the Chick. I'm going to run and meet Chase so we can go to that estate sale."

"No worries. I'm not planning to run the article until next week Wednesday with all the grocery ads. Have fun. I hope you find some nice furniture."

"I hope so too."

Laurie texted Chase that she was on her way. They met up at their apartment parking lot and Laurie hopped into the cab of his pick-up truck.

"What are these things?" she asked, moving aside two packages that were on the floorboard. They looked like some kind of brackets.

"Toss them into the back seat. Those are guitar hangers. I want to be able to get my instruments up off the floor. I'm going to pick some place in the new house where I can just hang them."

Laurie nodded as she set the hangers on the back seat. "I can't wait to see what furniture Don has for sale. Mary has been scouting her favorite thrift stores for me and sent me pictures of some kitchen tables, but I'm not over the moon about any of them."

They drove the short distance out of town to the home where Don and Alice had spent over twenty-five years. "This is it," Chase said, driving past the house to park in the first open spot he found.

"It's more modern-looking than I thought," Laurie said as they walked toward it. The house was a sprawling ranch, with wide double doors. "Modern in a mid-century sort of way. Look at the nice benches out here. I don't think we could fit anything else on our porch though."

"Let's remember our priorities. Something to sit on, and something to eat off of. If we find a bedroom set you're in love with I'll consider it, but I was really thinking of buying that new."

"Okay, okay. I'll try to be practical."

It didn't take long for them to walk through the house. Laurie stubbornly refused to look at any knick-knacks or china, although there was some pewter that caught her eye. The dining room set was already marked sold, but it was more formal than she had in mind. She and Chase both liked a trestle table with six lattice-back chairs in the country kitchen. There was a wide credenza in matching wood. "Would we use this as a buffet?" Laurie asked.

"Or in the living room, for storage." Chase ran his hand along the top, and then opened a cupboard below. "I could store my files in here."

"I'd say we could store china in it, except that we don't really have any. Plus there are so many cupboards in the kitchen, we wouldn't need the space." She checked the price and made a choking sound, looking wide-eyed at Chase. "What Don's asking is not really too bad, though. I've been looking at ads online, so I know what a set like this would cost brand-new."

They moved on to the living room, and Laurie pointed out a blue sofa with a tufted back and rolled arms. "What would you call this? Prussian blue?"

"I like it," Chase said. "You could pair it with red or rust. Or even light blue. Or yellow. Think Starry Night."

"You just like blue," Laurie smiled. "Maybe brick red, or red-red. Anyway, if you like it, it's okay with me. What I really like is this rug."

They continued through the house picking out a side chair, an end table, a few lamps, and a large painting of sailboats which Laurie fell in love with.

"You brought your check book, didn't you?" she asked finally.

"I did," Chase said. "You might want to step away so you don't have to hear how much money you spent today."

"I see some of our church friends in the kitchen. I'll go talk to them while you settle up."

Chase paid, and then rejoined Laurie. "All taken care of," he said. "And, I just called Buck at work. He has a trailer and said he would help me move this stuff tomorrow."

"And then you can go to Mary and Pete's place and pick up my stuff they've been storing in their garage."

"Speaking of work, I need to get back there pretty soon. Let's take the small things over to the house, and then tomorrow we can move the big stuff."

He and Laurie loaded the lamps, the rug, and a few other items into the truck, and made the short trip to Evergreen Drive to unload them in the living room. Laurie took a minute to unroll the rug before Chase reminded her he had to get back to work.

"Look, though," she said smiling. "It's less empty already. Before long we'll have to move my little desk here. That's when it'll really feel like home."

"And my guitars," Chase said, nodding.

* * *

Saturday morning early the moving started in earnest. Chase and Buck picked up the items from the estate sale. Then Chase drove the trailer over to Pete and Mary's house for Laurie's furniture. Mary had planned to help, but sent her regrets. Little Ricky was sick with a cold. Pete and Buck helped move the heavy items into the house on Evergreen Drive, and then left Chase and Laurie to finish setting things up.

As she puttered upstairs, Laurie could hear drilling and banging coming from the first floor. Finally she grew curious and went down to see what was going on.

She found Chase in the living room where he waved a hand proudly at the wall. "What do you think?" he asked, a bright smile on his face. The painting of Beebee hung above the credenza, along with three guitars.

Laurie felt her stomach sink as she looked from Chase to the wall. Slowly Chase's expression changed to worry. "What?" he asked, uncomprehendingly.

"Oh, Chase. I wish you would have asked before you put them up there." Her cell phone rang, and she slipped it out of her pocket to look at the screen, but replaced it without answering.

"But they look great there!" Chase said. "And look. There's the painting of Beebee. I love how it all comes together. The wood on the picture frame, the wood on the guitars ..." He looked questioningly again at her.

"But I wanted to hang the sailboat painting there!"

"I thought you wanted the painting on the long wall, above the couch. The colors kind of match."

"Argh!" Laurie made a guttural growl.

Chase looked at the wall and back at Laurie. Then he put his hands on his hips. "Do you want me to take it down? Because I will. I'll take it all down if it really makes you unhappy. I'll take the guitars upstairs. I'll put them in a closet." He folded his arms with a heavy sigh.

"Leave it," she said, shaking her head. "Maybe I'll get used to it."

"Look, I don't want you to be *miserable* every time you come into the living room."

She did feel miserable, and suspected she looked it. And Chase had looked so happy and proud when he invited her to inspect his handiwork.

She tried for a calmer voice. "No, really. I'm just ... surprised, that's all. I had thought of something different. But you're right. Probably the sailboats will go better above the couch. And this way your guitars will be handy, with your papers right here in the credenza. It's cool." Her phone rang again. She pulled it out and read the name on the screen. "Oh, Scott, what do you want?" she murmured before answering. "Hey, Scott. What's up?"

"You're not gonna believe this, but you might want to come meet me over at St. Mark's. The Tasty Chick is on fire."

Chapter 19.

"I'll be right there." Laurie said ending the call. Her mouth hung open and she stared at Chase.

"What? What is it?" he asked.

"That was Scott. The Tasty Chick is on fire. He's on the scene. Actually he's across the street at the church. Listen, I'm going over to St. Mark's. I don't know what I'll do, but maybe there's something." She looked again at the guitar wall, and then at Chase. "Leave this just as it is, okay? We'll talk some more later."

"You want me to go with you?"

Laurie thought for a moment, but shook her head. "No. Just keep working. I'll be okay. I'll let you know what's going on."

Laurie drove toward the church with a sick feeling in her stomach. Her thoughts kept flashing back to the sight of Bessie's son Anthony working on the fryer the morning of the interview.

She got as far as the Chinkapin Arts Center when she saw flashing lights and emergency vehicles ahead, and a policeman directing traffic around the area. She parked down the street, walking quickly the rest of the way. The Treasure Chest had already closed for the afternoon, and there were no cars in the church parking lot.

She found Scott and stood next to him gazing at the water all over the street, the soot-blackened building, and the people standing around. The building was still steaming, but it looked like the worst of it was over. "Do they know what happened?"

"I think so. Come this way, and you can get a better view." She walked with him along the road to where they could see the far end of the building. "Look there." He pointed to a gaping hole.

"Wow. I guess you took pictures already?" she asked.

Scott nodded gravely. "What a blow," he said. "I mean, this place is not just a restaurant, it's a Chinkapin institution. And I know what this means to the family. I read the article you drafted."

"Yeah, so much for my feature story," Laurie said. "Poor Bessie." She looked over to where Bessie stood talking to one of the firefighters. She was still wearing her chef's apron, but someone had draped a blanket over her shoulders. Two employees stood near her.

A car was waved through by the policeman, and pulled into the church lot. Bessie's son Anthony got out from the driver's side and rounded the car to open the door for an older man. Laurie guessed it must be Oliver. Leaning on a cane, he walked over to Bessie and put his arms around her. Laurie could tell now that the woman was sobbing.

Laurie shivered. "I didn't realize how chilly it was out here," she said to Scott. "I'm going to open up the church and make a pot of coffee. Why don't you let them know they can come in to the parish hall around back?"

Everyone in the church seemed to know the combination to the lockbox at the side door. Laurie dialed in the number, opened the door, and flipped on some lights. In the kitchen she filled the reservoir on the coffee maker, slipped in a jumbo K-cup, and slotted the carafe in place. As the water heated, she called Mother Barbara and filled her in on what was happening.

Coffee was still trickling into the carafe when people started trooping into the building. Bessie and her family found seats in the parish hall, and Laurie brought over the carafe and a stack of paper cups. She signaled Scott to join them, and introduced Bessie to her editor.

"Can you tell us what happened?" he asked.

"We were just cooking," Bessie said shaking her head. "Just cooking. It got a little smoky over by the fryer. That happens sometimes, when someone gets careless with the oil. But I opened the window, and the fan was on. Hazel was on the fryer. I was working on slaw, and we had Odette at the counter. Everything was going pretty good. Then Hazel started shouting. Well, by that time it was too late. I don't know if the fire started with the hot grease, or come up from the bottom, but it was everywhere. There was no putting it out." She looked at her husband. He patted her hand as a tear slide down her round cheek.

One of the firefighters walked over to their table. "Hey, Scott," he said, greeting the newsman.

"Hey, Brian. How does it look inside?"

"Hole in the ceiling. Hole in the wall. Water and smoke damage. The usual." The fireman seemed casual about the whole thing.

"Any idea what caused it?" Scott asked. He followed Brian away from the small knot clustered around Bessie. Laurie took a few steps in their direction to listen in.

"Probably a thermostat malfunction on the fryer, and the oil overheated and caught fire. That happens

if these commercial fryers don't get regular maintenance. Either that, or something happened with the
electric heating coils underneath the unit. Whatever
it was, the building's fire extinguishing system failed
to kick in."

Laurie glanced at Anthony, sitting gravely silent
beside his parents. Mother Barbara entered the parish hall, accompanied by additional stragglers from
the parking lot. The priest chatted with the restaurant employees waiting for rides home.

As the emergency personnel left the parish hall to
pack up, Laurie offered her condolences to Bessie
and her family. "You must be in shock. Is your son
taking you home?" She looked from Bessie to Anthony, and followed the family outside.

"We are going to fix this," Bessie said with cer-
tainty. "This is not the end of the Tasty Chick." She
looked at her husband and nodded. "I'm not letting
Oliver's restaurant end out this way. We are going to
fix this." She looked up at the building, where a fog-
gy dampness hung over everything.

"Come on Mama." Anthony wrapped the blanket
around her and looked sadly back at Laurie as he
walked his mother to his car.

Laurie returned to the kitchen to pour herself a
cup of coffee and text a quick update to Chase. Then

she rejoined the others in the parish hall. Barbara was still talking with Hazel, a tall woman with muscular arms, and Odette, a short, plump, motherly-looking woman. Both wore hairnets and Tasty Chick aprons.

"I've never worked anywhere else," Hazel said. "I don't want to work anywhere else."

Odette nodded. "Bessie's been like a mother to us. Both of us have had our problems, and she's helped us out every time."

"I don't know where I'll get the money for my electric and my water if I can't work," Hazel said. "I'll have to look for something else. But who's gonna hire me?"

"I done tried working somewhere else, and I didn't like it. I don't want to work with all them teenagers at the Hardee's or wherever. Those places don't pay nothing, and they want you to work until ten o'clock at night. I can't do that no more."

"You got that right," Hazel said. "I sure hope Bessie can fix the restaurant and re-open."

Laurie and Barbara exchanged a glance. "We'll keep that in our prayers," Barbara said.

* * *

The fire at the Tasty Chick was the talk of the parish hall after the service on Sunday morning. Quite a few people had heard the sirens the day before, and everyone saw the blue tarp over the end of the building across the street, and the caution tape crisscrossing the restaurant parking lot. Barbara told them what she had seen and heard. Others plied Laurie with questions knowing she worked for the local paper, and she obliged with answers, without hazarding an opinion about the cause of the blaze.

"It's the end of an institution," Phil, one of the parishioners, said.

"Well, don't put the nails in the coffin just yet," Laurie said. "I predict the Tasty Chick will rise from the ashes. The owners are determined to rebuild."

"That may be up to the insurance company," Barbara said grimly.

"Is there anything we can do to help?" Carol asked.

Her question was met with shrugs all around. "Let's think about that a while," Barbara said.

The next day an account of the fire ran on the front page of the *Journal*, with suspected causes, and a bit about the employees who were out of work. Laurie was surprised and a little annoyed thinking the feature she had put together had gone to waste, and went to talk to Scott about it.

"Don't worry. I'm using everything you wrote, and then some. Look at this." He rolled his chair over to the printer, pulled several sheets of paper out of the tray, and handed them to Laurie. "That's going to feature on the front of the foods section Wednesday."

Laurie nodded as she skimmed the pages. "This is great."

"Everything you wrote is in the midsection of the article. All I added was the stuff at the front, recapping about the fire, and telling how readers can donate to the rebuilding fund set up at the bank. We'll run another sidebar on the front page telling how to contribute."

"You old softie." Laurie smiled at Scott. "You must have set up that fund."

"It's not just altruism. I love those chicken tenders! I can't wait until the Tasty Chick re-opens."

"You're not the only one."

"We need to keep tabs on this story. I'm going to count on you to touch base with Bessie periodically, see how things go with her insurance claim, maybe even get her some help with that if needed. Our readers are going to want to know what's happening."

"You got it, boss."

Chapter 20.

Tuesday afternoon Laurie finished work at the paper and drove to the Treasure Chest to help out for a few hours. It was odd to see an empty parking lot across the street. Ordinarily at this time of day business would be brisk at the Tasty Chick. Now the blue tarp over the roof fluttered in the January chill.

Laurie was glad to find Carol working the counter. "Did you see the article in yesterday's paper about the Tasty Chick?" she asked, tossing her jacket and purse in the office.

"Sure did," Carol said. An odd smile played on her face.

"Wednesday's paper is going to carry a longer article, all about how the restaurant got started, and how people can contribute to the fund that's been set up at the bank to help rebuild. I sure wish there was something we could do to help. Maybe some Sunday Barbara could give the loose plate offering to the fund?"

"Mother Barbara is way ahead of you," Carol said. "I talked to her yesterday. One day a week for a month we'll donate Treasure Chest proceeds to the building fund. Most of the other volunteers have voted for Saturday. What do you think?"

"Sounds great to me. I think Saturday would be a good day. It's usually a busy day for us. We need to get the word out, and let customers know."

Laurie didn't waste any time making the announcement on social media. And it didn't take long for customers to notice. Even before the weekend, the Treasure Chest saw an increase in donations, and plenty of customers mentioned it when they came in to the shop.

By Friday Carol had to put out a plea for more help to deal with all the donated items. After her shift at the *Journal* and a quick lunch, Laurie went to the Treasure Chest to help get ready for what the volunteers knew would be a big day Saturday. Mary was already at work.

"I guess Ricky is feeling better?" Laurie asked.

"Yes. A lot better, I'm happy to say. And I can't wait to get over to your new house. Pete said it's starting to look good. But you probably haven't had much time to work over there, have you?"

"Not as much as Chase has, oddly enough. We still need to shop for a bedroom set. And I have to get you over there to show you how he decorated the living room." Laurie made a face, accompanied by a gagging sound.

"Not what you hoped for?"

"I don't know what I hoped for, but I'm fairly sure that wasn't it. And, I tried all those pretty keys Chase gave me for Christmas but none of them opened the mystery box."

"Bummer," Mary commiserated.

"I had one more key I wanted to try, but now I can't remember where I put it. Moving is such a pain. I can't find anything these days. Once we're settled in the new house I'm not going anywhere for a long time."

"I'm sure your key will turn up," Mary said. "Meanwhile, we've been tagging clothes all day, and something came in that you might be interested in." Mary crooned the last part in her little sing-song voice. Laurie knew when Mary 'sang' like that, it meant she was excited about something.

Mary led Laurie to the back of the shop where Evelyn was tagging clothing, and pointed to a dress lying on the work table.

It was a champagne-colored A-line dress with a boat neck, overlaid with shimmery lace. A row of crystal beads decorated the slightly empire waist. The sleeves were three-quarter length lace finished with a scalloped edge. It was a beautiful dress. "I think it might be your size," Mary said with a hopeful smile. "Why don't you try it?"

"I don't know," Laurie said. "I think my hips are too wide." She ran her fingers over the lace. She examined the crystal beading. She turned over the dress, lowered the zipper, and looked inside at the workmanship.

"That is a good-quality dress," Evelyn said. "I guarantee you that dress was expensive. I was going to put forty dollars on it."

"Forty!" Mary's jaw dropped. "We never mark our formals more than twenty. Twenty-five at the most, and then we end up giving most of them away to the high school for the prom dress drive."

"If they had that dress in Seven Sisters you know they'd mark it at least sixty," Evelyn said.

"They would," Mary said, her jaw tightening. "But this is *not* Seven Sisters." Seven Sisters was a classy consignment boutique in downtown Chinkapin. They carried only the best items, and their displays were gorgeous. But the Treasure Chest was not Seven Sisters, and the two shops usually had very different clientele.

Laurie said quickly, "Look, it doesn't matter how you price it. I don't even know if I'm interested." She laid the dress face up on the worktable and pulled at the skirt, checking the width. She gently stroked the crystal beads. "It is a pretty color, though. I'll try it on, just because it's here."

She grabbed the dress, walked to the fitting room and ducked inside the curtained booth. As she removed her slacks and sweater she could hear Mary grumbling just outside.

She threw the dress over her head. The skirt slipped easily over her hips, with just the right amount of flare to make it flattering without being loose. She reached back with both arms, wiggled around, and was able to slide the zipper up. She moved her elbows back and forth, checking for tightness in the shoulders. She smoothed her hands over the beaded waistline. Finally she looked at her reflection in the mirror, and a smile bloomed over her face. "Ma-ry," she called, and pulled the curtain aside.

Mary let out a little gasp. "Oh, Laurie, that is perfect. It fits like it was made for you." She giggled.

"You don't even have to lose fifteen pounds like most brides!"

"Good thing. I'll probably win the mega-millions before I lose fifteen pounds." Laurie stood back from the mirror and turned from side to side, admiring her reflection.

"Stay there. I have to take a picture for my Instagram. People will love that you found your wedding dress at a thrift shop." Mary headed toward the office to retrieve her phone from her purse, and nearly bumped into Evelyn as she came down the hall carrying a pair of men's shoes.

"You're seriously thinking of wearing a second-hand dress for your wedding?" Evelyn looked Laurie up and down. "Then again you're marrying a second-hand husband. Just 'second-hand Rose' all the way around." She tossed her head with a laugh and continued down the hall with the shoes.

Mary furrowed her brow as Evelyn disappeared into the men's clothing room. Laurie was frozen in front of the mirror; her face a bright red. Mary fidgeted nervously with her cell phone. It didn't look like the right time to take a picture. "Laurie?"

In a low, even voice Laurie said, "Unzip me, Mary."

"She's just being stupid. Typical irritating Evelyn," Mary said.

"Unzip this dress *now*," Laurie said again through
clenched teeth. Here hands were shaking. Mary
shoved her phone in her pocket and slid the zipper
down. Laurie disappeared into the changing booth.

A moment later she emerged in her sweater and
slacks. Tight-lipped, she grabbed her purse and coat
from the office.

"Are you leaving?" Mary asked.

"I can't talk now. Maybe later," Laurie said, and
pushed the door open, making the bells jangle loudly
against the glass.

* * *

Laurie strode down the sidewalk toward town, not
paying attention to where she was going. She was
seething. She didn't know what to think or say. If her
mind were clearer she might have thought of a snap-
py come-back to what Evelyn had said. But the
words "second-hand" kept ringing in her ears. "Second-hand husband."

She wore a second-hand engagement ring. She
drove a second-hand car. She had just tried on a sec-

ond-hand dress. Second hand. Second rate. Second class. Second best.

Laurie's feet pounded faster on the pavement. She wished she were at home where she could scream into a pillow. She would scream and scream and scream. It was a good thing she had left the thrift shop, because given a second chance she would shove a clothes hanger down Evelyn's throat. She would take a tagging gun and stab her in the heart. Laurie thought of a dozen creative ways to wreak vengeance on Evelyn, and was halfway to town before she turned around. She just wanted to get in her car and drive home.

She noticed Mother Barbara's car in the rector's parking space as she came abreast of the church. On impulse Laurie walked in at the side door that led to the church offices. She stood still, looking down the hallway toward the nave, and listened for sounds of life. She heard an office chair roll across the floor.

"Laurie! Come in," Mother Barbara called from her office. "It's good to see another living soul. It's been quiet here today."

Laurie walked into her office and sat in the visitor's chair, pulling her coat open. She was hot after walking so fast, and still breathing hard. "Working by yourself is not always a bad thing," Laurie said. "No one to piss you off."

"Ouch," Barbara said. "Not going well with a co-worker today?"

Laurie was silent for a moment. Finally she said, "That's putting it mildly. I don't know if *certain people* have to practice being jerks, or it just comes naturally. I used to like working at the Treasure Chest, but she's ruined it for me."

"I'm afraid to ask, because I'm sure it's someone I know," Barbara said. "Was it a friend?"

"This person has never been my friend, and will never be my friend. And if you start getting all 'love thy neighbor' on me, I'm going to get up and leave."

"I didn't say anything," Barbara said. "Just take some deep breaths and sit in that chair for as long as you like." Barbara got up and fetched a few papers out of the printer tray, punched holes with a three-ring hole-punch, and snapped them into a binder.

Laurie slouched down in the chair and folded her arms, watching as the priest puttered around the office. "Some people just have a way of making me feel so worthless; like such a failure. Like my whole life is second rate. I need someone to tell me I'm not a piece of dog doo-doo!"

"You are not a piece of dog doo-doo," Mother Barbara reassured her. Then she gave Laurie an appraising look. "It's never fun to feel criticized. And surely no one told you *that*."

"No, but I know that's what some people are thinking." Laurie scowled.

"You should listen to what you know in your own heart, and not what someone else says, especially if it's some hyper-critical person who you don't even care about. Sometimes when people spew crap it's more about them than about you. They have to put other people down, or have the best stuff, fly first class, or whatever it may be, because they're insecure or feel inferior. But you already know that. I've watched you grow over the last six months, and what I see is all in a positive direction. Life is good, isn't it? You're about to marry a wonderful man, and I think you've been moving into that new house?"

Laurie nodded. "Little by little."

"There. And that ring. I haven't really had a look at your lovely engagement ring."

Laurie held out her left hand. "It's second-hand, from the pawn shop. To go with my second-hand husband."

Barbara looked shocked. "Is that how you feel? Because I think it's lovely. Much prettier than the plain ones I usually see. And I think Chase is a lovely person. But as I said, it's not what I think, it's what you think. It's what you feel inside. You create your own reality."

"Whatever that means." Laurie pouted.

"If we were all perfect out of the box there would never be any growth or change. I'm not the person I was last year or five years ago. That doesn't mean I'm *used up*, or second best." She held her hand out, palm up and asked, "What do you want to do right now, this minute?"

Laurie took a deep breath and then let it out. "I want to go over to the Treasure Chest and buy the dress I tried on today. It fits me just right, it looks beautiful, and I want it for my wedding dress."

"Okay." Barbara nodded. "So what's stopping you? How long are you going to sit there obsessing over a careless remark from someone who doesn't matter?"

"Dang, you're a hard woman!" Laurie bounded out of the chair and was out the door in an instant. She strode across the parking lot and yanked open the door to the Treasure Chest.

Evelyn stood at the check-out counter. Laurie crossed her arms and leaned her elbows on the counter. "Have you tagged that dress yet? Because I'm buying it."

Mary appeared from the back. "Where were you? You disappeared, but your car was still here."

"I ran over to talk to Mother Barbara about something," Laurie fibbed. "And I was making my mind up about the dress, but I've decided to buy it."

Mary's face lit up. "I'll get it. I hung it with the formals." She scurried across the hall and came back with the dress on a hanger.

"It's a beautiful dress," Evelyn said simply. Laurie lifted her head and looked her in the eye, daring her to say more. She wondered if Mary had told her off, because Evelyn remained silent.

Mary grabbed a pen and the pad of sales tickets. "It's ... um ... forty dollars plus tax." She glanced nervously at Evelyn, and apologetically at Laurie.

"And worth every penny," Laurie said.

* * *

On Saturday business at the Treasure Chest was more than anyone had hoped for. Customers stood in the thrift shop parking lot and chatted quietly with their neighbors as they stared at the burned restaurant across the street. Then they came in and shopped.

Extra volunteers showed up at the shop to help, and it was a good thing. Two people worked the counter the whole day, writing up sales tickets, ringing them into the register, and wrapping and bagging items. Two other volunteers tagged and hung clothing, while a couple more sorted and priced miscellaneous donations that continued to pour in.

Chase arrived around noon with two sacks of Krystal hamburgers and a case of Cokes. He texted Laurie to come out to his truck and help carry them in.

"You're a doll," Laurie said giving him a quick kiss. "I didn't really want to eat peanut butter crackers again."

"I know Coke's not really your favorite either, so I picked up something else for you."

Laurie looked around expecting to see a Pepsi. Instead there was a tall latte in the truck's cup holder. Her face lit up. "For me?"

"You and nobody else but you."

"Will you marry me, Chase?"

"That's the plan," he said. He put his hands on her waist and kissed her again. "Grab one of those sacks. I'll get the rest."

Volunteers were glad to see Chase bringing food and drinks, and took turns grabbing a bite to eat.

At the end of the day Anne ran the totals on the cash register and the calculator. Then she ran them again on the calculator, with Virginia calling out the numbers from the sales slips. The others gathered around to hear the news. "Ladies, this is the first day we've made over a thousand dollars in the history of the Treasure Chest."

"And when you consider the things we sell are mostly just a buck or two, that's saying something," Virginia added.

"It's too bad we have to give it all to the Tasty Chick," Evelyn said, so quietly that Laurie was barely able to make out her words.

* * *

The next day at church Laurie wearily climbed the stairs into the choir loft, and joined Mary in the second row.

"I heard you had a big day yesterday," Mary said. "Sorry I couldn't make it to help."

"Yeah. I'm sure Mother Barbara will announce it during the service, but we made over a thousand dollars! We were on our feet practically the whole time."

"All for a worthy cause," Mary said.

Mother Barbara did announce the great sales day at the shop, and explained again about donating proceeds to help their neighbors across the street to rebuild. She showed pity on the exhausted volunteers by keeping her sermon short. Even with their choir rehearsal after the service, Laurie and Chase were out of the church before noon.

"I think we've beat the Methodists for a change. Want to stop at the Coffee Pot for a cinnamon roll? I promise I'll cook something more nutritious for supper."

"I think I need a cinnamon roll, for medicinal purposes," Laurie said.

They ordered, and sat at a quiet table in the back of the café. Laurie slumped in her chair and cradled a hot latte in her hands.

"You should have got an extra shot in that latte," Chase said. "You look tired."

"It's been a busy week. I was on my feet for hours yesterday." Laurie was tired, but it was more than physical exhaustion. She still felt the weight of Evelyn's comments bringing down her spirits.

Chase placed both hands over hers. "We could drive over to Springwood Gardens. There should be some beautiful camellias blooming now."

Laurie looked into his brown eyes, so full of tenderness, and studied his angular face. She had grown to love that face. "That sounds lovely, except I don't think my feet could take it right now."

"That's one of the things I love about you," he said.

"What? My feet?" She smiled, and pulled away from his hands to take a drink of her latte.

"No, the fact that you're willing to spend most of your Saturday on your feet in order to help out other people. Not everyone does that, you know. You didn't have to do that."

Laurie shrugged. If everyone just did one thing to help out someone else, the world would be a better place. Then again, she usually felt she didn't do enough. She hoped she could become the nice person Chase thought she was.

Chapter 21.

The following week things were a little more normal at the Treasure Chest. Maybe even slower than normal, due to the rain that wouldn't let up. Laurie drove to the *Journal* office in the rain Thursday morning. It was still raining at lunch time, and the rain showed no signs of slowing down as she pulled her car into the Treasure Chest parking lot that afternoon.

She tried without success to remember who the other cars in the lot belonged to. Finally she pulled her hood up and dashed inside. The bells jangled against the glass as the door swung shut behind her. "Hello," she called out hoping to see Carol. She was disappointed when Evelyn rounded the corner.

The woman was dressed as stylishly as ever in a coral long-sleeved top with a brocade vest and a boho beaded necklace. Laurie looked down at her own sweater and jeans.

That wasn't the only thing that crossed Laurie's mind. She was still angry over what Evelyn had said about her second-hand marriage plans. She hoped to escape into the back room where Joan and Anne were tagging clothes, and let Evelyn work the counter. Evelyn had other ideas.

"Look here. One of our regulars brought in all this jewelry, and now that our half-price sale on jewelry is over we can put it out, so let's tag it."

Laurie's hackles were up. She thought about telling Evelyn off and doing whatever she wanted, but some interesting jewelry caught her eye.

She took a seat and fished in the box, pulling out a couple of bracelets. "These are pretty," she said. "They match your top." She held them out, and looked up at Evelyn. On impulse she asked, "Evelyn, how tall are you?" Laurie thought she might be even taller than Chase. Chase had told her he was the shortest of three boys, a fact Laurie had verified again when she saw them all together after Christmas.

"I'm five-eleven in my stocking feet."

"Did you ever do any modeling?"

"Modeling was the last thing I wanted to do. I was too self-conscious when I was younger. I was the kid who hid from the camera." Laurie raised her eyebrows at that. "Here," Evelyn said. "Let's put three dollars on these. I'll find some card stock to clip these earrings onto."

Laurie had always thought Evelyn was an attractive woman, on the outside at least. And her posture was near perfect; not the hunch Laurie had developed from banging away on a laptop. She sat up a little taller, and caught sight of two women lingering outside.

In the shelter near the door the women shook water off their umbrellas and leaned them against the building before coming in. "Well, hey there, Evie, how are you?" One of the women smiled a little too sweetly, and gestured at Evelyn as she told her friend, "This is my old friend Evie Warren. She went to school with my baby brother."

"Good to see you Doris. Have you shopped with us before?"

"No. I've never been, but my friend told me I'd like this place. It belongs to your church next door, doesn't it?"

"Yes, that's right. Look around. We have clothing, décor, housewares, and all kinds of things. Just have fun exploring." Evelyn seemed anxious to push them along and get them away from the counter.

"Let's go back this way," her friend said. She looked vaguely familiar. Laurie was pretty sure Carol had introduced her once.

"Doris Kurzleben, you hag," Evelyn said under her breath when the women had gone on down the hall.

Laurie stared at Evelyn open-mouthed.

"Doris never forgave me for beating up her bratty little brother on field day in the fourth grade. If the little twerp had kept his mouth shut he would have been all right."

"What did he say?" Laurie asked, fascinated. This was a side of Evelyn she had never imagined.

"He kept taunting me, asking how many grades I had flunked."

Laurie's brow furrowed, and Evelyn clarified. "For the record, I never flunked. I was an 'A' student. I was also the tallest kid all the way through elementary and middle school, so somehow the rumor got around that I was older than the other kids and had flunked three grades. I straddled that kid and beat the snot out of him. Scraped up my knees to a fare-thee-well and was grounded for a week, but it was worth it."

"Wow," Laurie said. "I guess he had more mouth than brains, didn't he."

"Oh, yes he did. And he wasn't the only one. I gave another kid a black eye for asking me too many times 'How's the weather up there? How's the weather up there? How's the weather up there?' I really shouldn't have hit him so hard. I was sorry for that one, because otherwise he was a nice kid."

"I guess you had a hard time in school then, didn't you," Laurie said, writing a price on a tag attached to a necklace. Evelyn seemed awfully chatty for a change. Or maybe Laurie had never given her a chance.

"In school, out of school, everywhere. The school bus was the worst. The kids picked on me, so my mom and the bus driver made me sit up front. All that did was make me an easier target. I can still feel the spitballs on the back of my neck and on the side of my face. I had to pick them out of my hair. It was disgusting. I wore a hoodie all year long. It didn't matter if it was ninety degrees outside, I'd put the hood up and wear the thing like a veil down my back, to keep the spitballs off. I'd run around by the bus stop pulling straws and broken pens out of kids' pockets so they couldn't shoot spitballs at me, but then they just threw paper wads at me, so it didn't help much."

This didn't jibe with the picture of the indulged and pampered little girl Laurie had conjured in her mind. "Didn't your older brothers stick up for you at all?"

"Heck no. They were shorter than me!" She looked at Laurie, exasperated. "They were two grades ahead of me, but they were shorter than me. How ridiculous do you suppose that looked? No, I stayed away from them, especially in public. And they didn't want to hang around their baby sister anyway. I was left to fend for myself. Even the girls in school didn't want to be friends with me. They called me names when the teacher wasn't looking." Evelyn shook her head. Apparently it was not a pleasant memory.

"Like what?" Laurie asked.

"They called me the giraffe, so I used to put their stuff up on the top of the cubbies where they couldn't reach it. And then the teacher would call me out. I never got away with anything, but I tried.

"It wasn't just my height. I was a teacher's kid, and of course Father Tom was my grandfather. *Everyone* knew who I was, and every time I said 'boo' to some kid, word got back about it. I'd walk over to the church after school and help Grandma Ruth in the office and wait to see how long it would take for word to get around about what I'd done in school. Then I'd go home and shut myself up in my bedroom with Mollie, my dog, or take her out walking behind the house. I don't know what I would have done without her." She paused a moment. "I didn't have much to do with my brothers when I was a kid, but I sure loved that little dog."

Doris Kurzleben and her friend returned to the front of the shop. The friend placed a cookbook on the counter, and pulled out her wallet as Evelyn rang up the sale. "Doris, you didn't see anything you couldn't live without?"

"Not this time, dear. You certainly have some interesting items, but I really need to get rid of a few things before I bring anything else home."

"We take donations any time," Laurie chimed in. An almost inaudible snarl escaped from Evelyn's mouth, but she had her head down making change and the other women didn't hear.

Laurie waved the women off, and Evelyn watched through the door as they put up their umbrellas. "Goodbye, and don't come again soon," Evelyn said.

"Wow. Tell us how you really feel," Laurie said. She followed Evelyn's gaze.

"Oh, look. It's Donna and Melinda." Evelyn shook her head. "Nuh-uh, I think her mother was right.

Donna is farther along than she said. Just look at her."

The bells on the door jangled and a pair Laurie recognized from several months ago entered the shop. Donna's pregnant belly jutted out from her open jacket. The girl looked about ready to pop.

"Hello again." Evelyn greeted them with a smile. "It's good to see you. How have you been?"

Something had changed between mother and daughter. They both were looking much happier than last time. The girl laid a hand on the counter, and Laurie noted a diamond ring on her finger.

"We're coming along," Melinda said looking at her daughter. "We're here to see what you have for decorating a nursery. Someone just gave us a nice used crib. Another month and the baby will be making her *or his* appearance."

"I'm telling you, Mom, it's a girl. I can feel it," Donna said.

Melinda rolled her eyes. She and Donna argued as Evelyn led them down the hall toward the linens room.

Laurie tagged jewelry while they shopped. She wondered if Donna's boyfriend had reappeared and they were now engaged, or if the ring was just for show, to keep people from asking questions. Either way, the girl was obviously excited about the baby, and that made Laurie happy. She was glad Melinda was there to help her daughter.

Laurie's baby-fever had subsided, with all the excitement she felt over her own engagement and her new house. Still, she could feel it stir again when she saw a pregnant woman or a cute baby.

Finally Evelyn led the mother and daughter back to the counter carrying crib bumpers and other items. Melinda lugged a car seat, and Donna carried an armload of onesies, sleepers, and bibs. Laurie grabbed the sales receipts to start writing.

"This will be eight," Evelyn said.

Laurie scratched out twelve dollars which she had just written down for the linens, and changed it to eight. Then she wrote up the clothing items as tagged. "What about the car seat?" she asked.

"We never charge for those," Evelyn said. "The state keeps changing their rules on safety requirements, so we can't really guarantee them. I happen to know that one's less than a year old, though."

"Well it looks really new," Melinda said. "Anyway, it's an extra to go in my husband's car, just in case." Melinda paid the bill, and she and her daughter walked out of the store with twenty or thirty dollars-worth of stuff (by thrift shop standards) for just twelve dollars.

Laurie looked appraisingly at Evelyn. "What?" Evelyn asked.

"Nothing," Laurie said shrugging. She tried to compose her face, but a spiteful smile touched her eyes. "I guess you have a heart after all. Or maybe you just have a soft spot for infants."

Evelyn put her nose in the air and looked away. Then she turned back to Laurie. "Infants in distress, young mothers, and stray dogs. You probably don't know that I was adopted."

At last Laurie's suspicions were confirmed. She was surprised by the sharpness in Evelyn's voice. The woman looked defiant, but then the starch seemed to go out of her.

"Before you ask, I don't know who my birth mother was, or why she didn't want me. And then dad left us when I was young. It all made me very angry."

"I thought I heard your father *died* young," Laurie said, uncertain.

"Left. Died. Same thing. I was in kindergarten at the time. I didn't understand cancer. I just knew he was gone, and then mom went to work and was gone all the time too."

"And no one could tell you anything about your birth mother? I mean, can't your mother tell you anything?"

"When I was younger I figured if my birth mother didn't want me I didn't want to have anything to do with her either, or know anything about her. My grandparents tried to tell me one time, and I wouldn't let them. Of course the older I got the more I realized she might not have had a choice. Now my grandparents are gone, and Mom's in that memory care unit at the nursing home."

Laurie's reporter sense was aroused. She wanted to know more about this story, and wondered whether adoption records were sealed in Georgia.

"I've tried asking Mom about when I was born, but she gets all fidgety and anxious, and won't say anything. I've seen photos of her pregnant, and I know the pictures were taken after the twins were born. I think she lost a baby and then adopted me, but that still doesn't tell me anything. I don't know who arranged the adoption, or if I was even born in Georgia."

Suddenly it was as if a spigot had been turned off. Evelyn was all business again, and didn't share any more personal information. "How are you coming with the jewelry? Go ahead and tag what's in this box

too. I put it away when we had the old stuff on sale."
She brought out another box of items and suggested
some prices.

Laurie continued tagging jewelry until the box
was empty. Evelyn helped a customer who wanted to
buy the outfit off a manikin, and then she re-dressed
the manikin with new clothing.

Finally Anne and Joan came out of the back room,
ending Laurie's chance to ask Evelyn more questions. Anne offered to help Evelyn cash out, and Laurie and Joan walked out of the shop chatting
together.

"How's your new house coming along? And when
are you going to move?" Joan asked.

"It's coming along great. We've got most of the
downstairs set up, and parts of the upstairs. We plan
to move in right after our wedding. The night of, actually. Provided we buy a bedroom set, that is. I
found a beautiful set yesterday afternoon, and I'm
taking Chase to see it this evening."

"Well, good luck then. See you soon."

Chapter 22.

Laurie arrived at Chase's apartment to find him already working on supper. She watched him toss together greens and other vegetables in a salad bowl. She rummaged in the fridge for some black olives and placed them on the counter. "Thanks, Babe," he said, and gave her a kiss. "Want to throw some pasta into the pot?" He indicated the pot of water bubbling on the stove.

Laurie tossed in handfuls of pasta and set the kitchen timer. She lifted the lid on a small saucepan filled with a creamy concoction, and closed her eyes as she took a deep breath of the steamy air, fragrant with romano and parmesan cheese. She tried to imagine what it was going to be like in their new kitchen on Evergreen, but honestly could not imagine it being better than this.

Finally Chase poured the sauce over the steaming pasta and placed the bowl on the table. "It smells so good. I love your cooking."

"Just wait until our wedding feast. Mwa-ha-ha."

Laurie paused with a forkful of pasta halfway to her mouth. "That evil laugh has me worried. Have you come up with a new menu? Instead of barbecue are we having, I don't know, rattlesnake or something?"

"I want it to be a surprise. Now eat. We have shopping to do."

* * *

Laurie woke on Saturday to two sounds she loved: the sound of rain against the window pane and Chase clanging pots and pans. She pulled the covers away from her head. Pale morning light filtered around the edges of the window blinds, and the smell of frying bacon mingled with the faint whiff of coffee. She threw on her robe and wandered into the kitchen, looking hopefully toward the coffee pot.

"Arise my love, my fair one, and come away," she said, her hand extended toward the pot.

"Here," Chase said handing her an empty mug. "You might need one of these."

"Bless you my child." She poured herself a cup and sipped. "Ahhh. My favorite things. You and coffee. Not necessarily in that order."

"'You and me and rain on the roof,'" Chase sang, bopping around the small kitchen. "Quick. Tell me who used to sing that."

"Umm." Laurie gazed pensively at the ceiling. Then she shook her head. "Who am I kidding? I have no idea."

"The Lovin' Spoonful."

"Gaah. It was on the tip of my tongue."

"Liar," Chase said. "But now, cheese grits: those can be on the tip of your tongue." He spooned some grits onto a couple of plates that already had servings of scrambled eggs and bacon on them, and put the plates on the table.

Laurie looked at the pot on the stove. "You sure made a lot of grits. Are we expecting company for breakfast? Should I put some real clothes on?"

"I saw a recipe for fried cheese grits balls that I wanted to try. Might be something good for our wedding."

"Chase, you're torturing me. Why?"

He grabbed her hand and kissed her fingertips. "Darlin' Laura May it's because you look so cute when you're aggravated!" He dropped her hand and scooped up a forkful of grits.

"Why does everything have to be fried? Fried Twinkies. Fried tacos. The worst thing I ever tasted in my life was fried dill pickles. Yuck!"

"Well, I thought you wanted finger foods at your wedding reception. This recipe makes grits a finger food."

"You forgot the scrambled eggs. How are you going to make them a finger food?"

"Oooh! We could have deviled eggs! Thanks for the idea."

Laurie slapped her forehead with the heel of her palm a few times. "Why? Why? Why am I being punished like this?"

Chase just laughed. "Eat your eggs before they're cold. I have to go get Buck's trailer so we can pick up our new bedroom furniture." They ate silently for a few moments. "After we move the furniture maybe I'll do a few other things at the house. Are you sure you want me to leave the guitars on the wall?"

"Yes. I'm resigned. I think they look fine, actually." She was still thinking about food. "I saw in the paper that there's a sale on pork butts at the grocery," she said casually.

"That's nice. Do you have a craving flung on you for a pork butt?" Chase asked. His eyes sparkled and a smile tugged at the corners of his lips.

"I just thought you might need to start stockpiling, if we're going to have barbecued pork at the wedding," she said.

"I've got the food for the wedding well in hand. Don't you worry about a thing."

Laurie growled at him. "You like to keep me in suspense, don't you," she said. "You know I can't stand not knowing."

"You trust me, don't you?" he said, reaching for her hand.

She squinted at him and then breathed a sigh. "I suppose so. But if I don't like it, I'll ..." She gazed into his brown eyes, so full of laughter. She adored this man. If he served cheese curls and pork rinds, well, she'd be annoyed at that, but she would forgive him.

"You'll what?" he asked, daring her to come up with something.

"I'll stuff myself with wedding cake until my eyes pop out."

"Oh, you wanted a cake at the wedding?" he asked, feigning innocence. "Stuff yourself with wedding cake. That would show me! But never fear. You won't have to do that. I promise. Now eat your breakfast. We have to get busy if we're going to move into our house by the first of March."

* * *

After church Sunday Chase and Laurie went out to lunch with Pete and Mary, and Chase insisted on picking up the tab. "This is to thank you for helping us move our new furniture," Chase told Pete.

Laurie nodded. "If we'd waited for the store to deliver it, it would have taken two weeks, plus the forty dollar delivery fee. I spent all yesterday afternoon getting it set up."

"I can't wait to see it," Mary said. "I'm sorry I wasn't there to help. I had to watch the little one." She smiled her impish smile. "That's my new excuse any time hard work rears its ugly head. 'But I have to watch the baby.'" She opened her mouth wide, and spooned more mashed peas into Ricky's mouth.

"Come and see our house this afternoon," Laurie invited her. "I'll be there hanging curtains. Plus we have lots to catch up on." With so many people around at church, Laurie hadn't told Mary what she'd learned about Evelyn's childhood.

"I'd love to. Pete's playing golf later today. If I can get a sitter for a couple of hours, I'll meet you there."

* * *

Second Home

A short while later Laurie opened the front door of 501 Evergreen Drive and ushered Mary in. Mary paused in the foyer to slip off her shoes. Then she straightened as Laurie pointed into the living room with a flourish.

"Voila. The guitar wall." She rolled her eyes with a grimace and waited for Mary's reaction.

Mary stood with hands on hips. "Quite a departure from your first home."

"Yeah, but none of the stuff in that house ever meant anything to me. DB wanted it decorated like out of a magazine, and hired a decorator to do it. It wasn't personal. It didn't reflect anything about me, or us, or even about him except how important status was to him. But this!" Laurie gestured again to the wall. "It kind of hurt my eyes at first."

"Well, girlfriend, if you want personal, this is it. Chase is all about music and guitars. And you've told me how much you enjoy listening to him play and sing." She looked around and took in the whole room. "Still, he could have asked you before he hung his guitars in the living room."

"Well," Laurie hesitated. "He did kind of ask me, but I guess all I heard was that he was going to put the painting of Beebee in the middle."

"I know you think it's weird, but really this is *not* that weird. Remember, I was a music major. I've seen this type of thing lots of times."

"Really?"

"Oh, yeah. Lots of people decorate with musical instruments. And you can buy guitar hangers with all kinds of quotes from famous guitarists on them. You should be happy that Beebee is there in the middle, instead of some quote by Eric Clapton."

Laurie shook her head and sighed. "Sometimes I'm just not sure. I wish we could agree on things."

Mary cocked an eyebrow at her. "Too late to cancel the wedding now. I already got my invitation. You probably just have pre-marital jitters. Everyone gets them. Plus your last marriage turned into such a disaster. Anyway, what are you not agreeing about?"

"The food for the wedding. Although I guess I'm over that," Laurie said as she led Mary up the stairs. "He wants traditional southern food, which wasn't what I had in mind, but I'm having a hard time arguing with him. I was leafing through a *Southern Living* wedding edition the other day, and one of the suggested menus was chicken and waffles with mac 'n' cheese and sweet potato soufflé."

"Yum. Sounds good," Mary said.

"You're supposed to be on my side!" Laurie glared at her. "Next thing I know you'll be suggesting banana pudding instead of wedding cake."

"Watch out there. You're treading on some sacred cows."

"I really don't care anymore. As long as it's not pork rinds and hot sauce. Here's the spare room." Laurie flourished a hand as Mary nodded in recognition at some of the pieces from Laurie's childhood bedroom set.

"What else have you two been disagreeing about?" Mary asked.

"The guest list."

Mary folded her arms. "What?? Who did he want to invite that you didn't?"

"Everyone in the church."

Mary took a step back. "And that's a problem because...? You two have a lot of friends there. You *met* there." Then she narrowed her eyes. "Oh. I know who it is. It's Evelyn, isn't it."

Laurie wrinkled her nose and nodded.

"Oh, jeez. I'm not even gonna go there. Look, I've got one more hour on my babysitter. Show me your new bedroom set, and then we'll go shop for you a pair of shoes."

They retreated down the hall and Laurie proudly showed off her bedroom. "I'm happy with the way this room turned out." It was light, airy, and comfortable-looking. The large windows overlooking the back yard were hung with shimmery, pale silk curtains, which added a look of luxury without making the room overly feminine. "Listen to how quiet it is in this house. There's no traffic noise."

"Just wait. In a month or so all the lawnmowers and leaf blowers will be out."

Laurie stuck out her tongue. "Come on. You have to see my boudoir with the vanity and wardrobe I got from the antique mall."

Mary admired the furniture, and the chandelier hanging from the ceiling in the little room. Laurie's wedding dress hung on the open door of the wardrobe. "You are going to look gorgeous," she crowed. "And I like your slipper chair by the window. You don't mind if I put some pictures on Instagram, do you? These will be great for *Affordable Elegance.*"

Mary took out her phone and snapped a few pictures. "But you're not officially moving in until the wedding?"

"Nope. We can't get out of the leases on our apartments until then. Plus I'm saving my *new* home for my *new* life with my *new* husband."

"That sounds nice when you say it that way."

"Right," Laurie nodded. "Not second, like second-hand or second-rate. *New.*"

Mary took a seat in the slipper chair and looked happily around the room. Laurie pulled open the door to the cupboard closet to show her the shelving Chase had installed inside.

"Oh!" Mary exclaimed suddenly. "Where's your box?" She dug in her purse and handed Laurie a small key made of dull brass. The top was heart-shaped, with a crown in the center. "*This* was way down in the pocket of that purse you donated to the Treasure Chest. I found it Friday."

Laurie's eyes widened. "That's the key I lost! The one from Barbara's office. Maybe it's the one." She grabbed the wooden mystery-box from the cupboard and sat on the small vanity bench with the box on her lap. Her heart pounded as she slid the key into the keyhole. "Ooh, that felt good," she said smiling. Mary giggled.

She had to use some force, but finally the key turned with a gritty little click. Laurie tugged on the lid, and the box was open.

Chapter 23.

Mary scooted nearer to look inside the box as Laurie removed a small bundle wrapped in tissue paper. Beneath it were a few old photographs and folded papers. While Mary looked at the photos, Laurie gently opened the tissue.

A small gasp escaped her. Wrapped in the tissue paper was a baby bonnet decorated with citrus colored ribbons of lemon-yellow, tangerine, and lime. She looked at Mary wide-eyed. "It's Evelyn's!"

"And look here," Mary said holding up one of the photographs. It was the same image that they had seen in the old photo album at the Treasure Chest, of baby Evelyn in her mother's arms and wearing the bonnet.

"Mary, I have something to tell you," Laurie began, and filled her friend in on everything Evelyn had told her. "But why is this here, at my house?" Laurie asked finally.

Mary pulled a folded piece of paper from the box. "It's a birth certificate. 'Eva Janelle Rutherford'," she read. "Is that our Evelyn? The mother's name is Kimberly Michelle Rutherford. No father's name listed."

Laurie picked up one of the letters and began reading.

Dear Kim – Please put your mind at rest about letting Nancy adopt your baby. The boy's parents are not going to make any claim on Eva. I doubt he even told them you were pregnant. And now that he's gone they'll never need to know. I hope from now on you'll stay away from boys with motorcycles!

"Okay, slow down," Mary said. "I'm trying to figure out who they're talking about."

"Nancy is Evelyn's mother. Adopted mother, I mean. And Kim, or Kimberly, as the birth certificate says, must be the birth mother. And the letter is talking about the boy's parents. Maybe Kim was worried they would want the baby? I'm not sure what it means, about the motorcycle." Laurie continued reading.

Bottom line, the boy's family is out of the picture.

And you couldn't keep the baby. Not after Jackie died – you know that in your heart. A sixteen-year-

old doesn't need to be raising a baby all alone. And your parents couldn't raise it either. What would everyone say, after all your mother's purity pledge work, if her own daughter showed up with a bastard? Because that's what people would call Eva. You don't want your child and the rest of your family to live with that!

You are doing my Nancy a favor, giving little Eva to her. No one has to know her own baby was still-born, although we are grieving for our little angel. Of course we'll keep everything quiet. Tommy will do a private service and scatter the baby's ashes at the church. All anyone will know is Nancy went into the hospital pregnant and came out with a baby girl. It's what she wanted, after the two little boys. I really see the hand of God in all this. So if you call what you're doing 'abandoning' one more time I'm going to take Eva myself and give her to the gypsies!

Kim, trust me. This is the best for all. Eva will have a loving home and two big brothers to look after her, and now you can get on with your life, finish high school, and go travel around Europe for real instead of making up stories about it while you hide out with your aunt in Calhoun.

All my love to you. I know your heart will ache for ·a while, but this is truly for the best.

Ruth T.

"Ruth. That has to be Reverend Thigpen's wife," Laurie said. "And *his* name was Tom. Tommy. He did the funeral service for the baby who died, and scattered her ashes at the church."

"That's right. Ruth and Tom Thigpen were Evelyn's grandparents." Mary nodded.

"Adopted grandparents," Laurie said. "Because Evelyn's birth mother was Kim Rutherford."

"And Nancy, Evelyn's adoptive mother, was Ruth's daughter," Mary said as her eyes lit up. "Nancy was pregnant and her baby was stillborn, or died somehow. So she adopted Kim's daughter, Eva. It's all making sense."

"All except why this box of stuff is in my house," Laurie said again.

"The people you bought the house from. What was their last name?"

"Their name was Hinsdale. Oh!" Laurie's eyebrows climbed as she looked wide-eyed at Mary. "But Chad told me they'd bought it from someone named Rutherford." She picked up the birth certificate and looked at it again. "He said the Rutherfords were all gone from Chinkapin. I don't remember if they died, moved away, or what."

"What else is in the box?" Mary asked.

Laurie rifled through it, and opened another letter. "It's from Ruth to Kim again." She skimmed the letter. "Oh, I think it's talking about the bonnet. Listen to this."

Dear Kim,

I'm sending this to you, since you purchased it for the baby. I thought you would like it as a keepsake. I'm enclosing a few photos as well.

Baby Evelyn (that's what Nancy insists on calling her) is doing well. We all love her, and the twins dote on her. She is growing like a weed! She will be tall like the Rutherfords. Maybe a model or an actress.

I'm so glad to hear that you are back in school. Blessings and love to all your family and especially to you. We are forever grateful.

Yours, Ruth

"So, does Evelyn know that your new house is where her birth mother lived?" Mary asked.

"I told you, she doesn't know *who* her birth mother was," Laurie said. "You know, she said outright that she was adopted, so I'm guessing other people must know, even though everyone I asked wouldn't say anything. It's all been kind of strange."

"What are you going to do with the box?"

"That's a good question, Mary. A very good question."

* * *

"Let's forget about shoe-shopping," Laurie said a short while later. "I'm just not up to it. Let's go get a coffee instead."

"I can tell it's going to be dangerous for you, living so close to the Coffee Pot," Mary said.

"You can drive us there, and I'll walk back to the house. That way, if I accidentally eat a cinnamon roll it won't all stick to my hips."

"Okay, but you better give me a bite. And I can't stay too long. I only have thirty more minutes on my baby-sitter meter."

At the Coffee Pot they each ordered a cappuccino and got a pecan square to share, since the café was out of cinnamon rolls. While they ate they discussed the contents of the box.

"It kind of sounded like Ruth Thigpen engineered the whole adoption business so her daughter would have a baby girl," Mary said.

"Or just a baby," Laurie said. "I don't know that the sex mattered. We know Nancy had been pregnant and apparently lost a baby, so maybe she was in on it too. Or maybe Ruth was just really trying to do Kim and Nancy both a favor. It sounds like she was friends with Kim's family. Remember she talked about Kim's mom, and her aunt in wherever it was."

"Calhoun," Mary said.

"Wherever. Kim and her family were keeping the pregnancy quiet. They probably would have put the baby up for adoption regardless." Laurie looked thoughtful for a moment. "It must have been so hard for her, first of all to be pregnant so young, and then to give her child away."

"It must have been. But also hard for Nancy, since her baby died. You know, she never gets out of that nursing home these days. She must be really bad off." Mary rose and snapped the lid on her drink. "I have to hit the road. Are you going to call Evelyn?"

"That hag. I should just burn the box."

Mary looked shocked. "You're not going to do that!"

"Maybe. Maybe not. Or maybe I'll just surprise her with it one of these days. I'd kind of like to see her expression. I have to think about it."

Mary raised her eyebrows at that. "Just don't think too long."

* * *

Laurie drained her cappuccino and left the café for some window shopping. She wanted to walk and think. She paid little attention to things passing in front of her eyes. Her mind was on the items now locked back in the box, and the revelation it contained. She would have to give it to Evelyn. But she was in no hurry. Evelyn had irritated her so much, and so often. The woman could wait.

Laurie was so deep in thought that someone called her name twice before she even looked up. She was surprised to see Bessie coming toward her on the sidewalk.

"Bessie! I'm glad to run into you. I've been meaning to call you. How is everything going?" She felt guilty for not checking in with her, because she was a friend, and because Scott had wanted a follow-up article for the *Journal*.

"I'm doing well. Been fighting with the insurance, but I think I got about all the blood I'm going to get out of that turnip. I sure do appreciate the money from the Treasure Chest, Laurie, and just everything you've done for me. You and that darlin' Chase of yours."

Laurie felt her face turning red. "It was just an article, Bessie. Other people did more than I did, with the rebuilding fund and all. I hope it's enough to re-open your restaurant."

"I believe we'll be able to open the Tasty Chick again soon. I can feel it." She had a satisfied smile on her face. Laurie was a little mystified, but glad to see Bessie so hopeful.

"What else have you been up to?" Laurie asked.

"I'm working at the bakery over there at Publix, but I'll be glad when I can finally quit. I just can't get up so early anymore! Their people have to be there at the crack of dawn. I mean *way* before the rooster crows. I'm not made for getting up so early. But that's all right." She smiled again.

"Well good. Glad to hear it," Laurie said.

"I got to get on home to Oliver. But I thank you again. Take care of that sweet man of yours. He really is a treasure, and so are you."

Laurie waved goodbye, wondering at the woman's gratitude. If anything, Laurie felt like she hadn't done enough. Lately she had been absorbed in her wedding clothes, and buying things for the new house, and nursing petty injuries like Evelyn's careless remarks and Chase's guitar wall.

Bessie was right about Chase. He really was a treasure. Laurie knew she was lucky to have him. He was always so even-tempered, in spite of the mistrust and jealousy she'd shown in the past.

Laurie wondered if anyone thought of her as a treasure. Certainly not Evelyn! Evelyn had so many unanswered questions. And what reason, other than spite, did Laurie have for holding on to the box, which contained Evelyn's bonnet and the answers she'd been seeking for so long?

The choir at St. Mark's had practiced an anthem for Ash Wednesday, and now a line from the song popped into Laurie's mind. It was something based on one of the psalms, and it had resonated with her at the time because she was trying to prepare herself for her new life. Now she thought of it again.

Create in me a clean heart, O God,
And put a new and right spirit within me

Laurie knew that if she was going to start her new life in her new home with a clean heart and a right spirit, then giving Evelyn what rightfully belonged to her was part of the deal. And since there was less than a week until the wedding, it had to be soon.

Second Home

She made up her mind to give Evelyn the box the following week.

* * *

Laurie had a lot of last-minute arrangements for her wedding: among other things, a meeting with Mother Barbara and Chase to be sure the ceremony was all planned, and a get-together with Mary who offered to help Laurie figure out a hairstyle for the big day. Chase assured her that he was handling the food and the music for the wedding. She would just have to trust him. And if she didn't, why on earth was she marrying him?

Finally she just turned it all over to God and the people she loved, and tried to relax.

Meanwhile, Mary did a little reconnaissance for her, and found out Evelyn was definitely working at the Treasure Chest on Friday. Mary would also be there. Laurie put the box in her car Thursday afternoon, and drove to the Treasure Chest straight from work on Friday. She planned to find a moment alone with Evelyn to give her the box in private.

Mary had just left the shop, leaving the two alone, when Laurie realized that the box was locked and the key was still at the house on Evergreen Drive. As she frantically tried to get Mary on the phone, the bells on the door of the Treasure Chest jangled. Laurie was surprised to see Carol. "I thought you couldn't make it today. Mary said you had some emergency."

Carol put a hand to her hair. "My hair stylist had the emergency. She wanted to go out of town this weekend, and bumped my appointment to today instead of Saturday. It just shows how fast she can work when she sets her mind to it. I knew if I didn't get my hair colored now I would have to find someone else or do it myself. Last time I did that I ruined three bath towels."

"It looks nice," Laurie said, admiring Carol's short teased hairstyle and sweeping bangs.

Carol smiled as Evelyn came in with an armload of blouses. "I made it," Carol said to Evelyn. "Laurie, you can go on home now, if you want."

Laurie thought quickly. "I'm going to run out for a bite of lunch. I'll be back in a while."

"Go ahead, then," Evelyn said. "It probably won't get very busy until later this afternoon."

Laurie drove straight to Evergreen Drive, dashed upstairs, and fetched the key to the box from her boudoir.

She ran down the stairs again and almost knocked Chase over. "Oh! I didn't know you were here. I came for this. I need to give it to its rightful owner." She furrowed her brow. "What are you doing here? I thought you'd be home making grits bits, or something."

"The grits balls didn't work out. They kept crumbling apart."

"Aw. Such a shame," Laurie said with a smirk.

"I'll have to come up with something else. Maybe gator bites."

"Yuck," she said shaking her head and moving toward the kitchen. "Well, I didn't have lunch. Do we still have some snacks here?" She opened the pantry to snag a couple of food bars, and stared wide-eyed. "Where did all this food come from?"

"I guess the food fairies must have been here," Chase said innocently.

"Chase, are there a dozen pork butts in the freezer?" She was suddenly suspicious.

"No. Cross my heart and hope to die, stick a pork butt in my eye. Seriously, when I carry you over the threshold after we're married I don't want to have to carry you back out again so we can go buy groceries."

"You are a doll, Chase Harris. I can't wait to marry you." Laurie gave him a big kiss on the cheek, feeling very happy all of a sudden. He pulled her into a hug, and didn't let her go for several moments.

Laurie drove back to the thrift shop, and waited nervously for the right opportunity to speak to Evelyn. She never got a chance until closing time. She puttered back and forth, shutting off lights and setting the thermostat while Evelyn and Carol totaled the money in the drawer and updated the books. Luckily everything balanced on the first go-around, and the three women walked out together.

"I'll see you in church. I'm looking forward to that wedding," Carol called before driving off.

"Evelyn, I have something to show you." Laurie beckoned her over to her car, which was parked next to Evelyn's. "It's something I found while Chase and I were working at our new house."

Evelyn looked mystified. "Where is your new house again?" She pressed the button on her fob to unlock her car, and tossed her purse onto the seat.

"It's on Evergreen. Number 501." The address didn't seem to mean anything to her. "We bought the house from the Hinsdales, but before them it was owned by people named Rutherford."

At the mention of the name Evelyn's eyes widened. "Oh, really! My grandma Ruth was friends with a Jane Rutherford. Her daughter Miss Kim used to babysit me sometimes, but they moved to California."

Laurie reached inside her car, withdrew the box from the back seat, and handed it and the key to Evelyn. "I think the things inside are yours."

Evelyn opened the box and lifted the tissue paper to reveal the bonnet. Mechanically she set the box down on the hood of the car. Her hands shook as she pulled the bonnet free of the paper.

"Oh, my God." Her mouth turned downward. Her lips trembled and tears shimmered in her eyes. "This *is* mine." She turned it over and over in her hands, stroking the ribbons, and brushed a tear off her cheek.

She nestled the bonnet back into the tissue and pulled out some of the papers.

"There's something about your birth mother in there," Laurie said.

Evelyn looked at her, eyes shining. She looked down at the photos, and then unfolded one of the letters. "Grandma Ruth," she whispered. "I'll have to look at these at home." She tucked them back in the box. Then she shocked Laurie by throwing an arm around her shoulder and hugging her. "Thank you. I'm so happy to have these. They mean ... they mean so much to me."

Laurie smiled mutely. Then she slid behind the wheel of her car and drove away without looking back.

Chapter 24.

Laurie hurried to answer the knock on her apartment door, but paused before opening it. "Who is it?"

"Open the door or I'm keeping this latte for myself," Mary answered.

"Is it a plain latte?" Laurie asked.

"Seriously? It's your wedding day. It's a Southern Classic. Now open the door so I can help you get beautiful."

Laurie stood behind the door, cracking it open to let her friend in. "Mary, I am so, so nervous!" She stood in her slip and panty hose, waving her hands in front of her.

"Calm down, girlfriend." Mary set her dress bag and a small cosmetics case on the couch. "How much coffee have you had this morning?"

"Not enough."

"Well, have you eaten anything?"

"No. I just finished drying my hair and putting on make-up."

"I figured," Mary said, opening a bag on the kitchen table. "That's why I stopped at the Coffee Pot and got some actual food."

"Bless you, you are an angel!" Laurie dove at the bag, pulled out the bagel and cream cheese, and started munching.

Mary watched as her friend ate. "I like your nail polish."

Laurie took a moment to admire her fingernails. "I usually don't bother, but this is a special occasion." She raised her eyebrows and smiled. "I came home yesterday after working at the thrift shop, and haven't even talked to Chase. We've texted a few times, so I know he'll be at the church when we get there. I can't wait to see what he's wearing. Probably that same old suit he wore to the funeral in November." She wrinkled her nose. "I hope he has a new tie."

"We'll know in another couple of hours. You'll be happy when you see the church. I checked everything out yesterday. The ladies from the flower guild did the alter flowers, and put two little bouquets on either side of the aisle at the ends of the first pew. You know, not too much, but made it look pretty. And your bouquet is in the flower cooler."

"How does it look?" Laurie asked around a mouthful of bagel.

"You'll like it. It's so pretty. Stephanotis, lily of the valley, and roses, some white and some a sort of blushy-peach. It should look nice with your dress."

"No gardenias?"

"I asked Dot, and she said the smell would be too strong. Since Chase has allergies, and you didn't want silk flowers, they went with the lily of the valley instead. It smells nice, but not overpowering."

Laurie threw her wrapper and napkin away and took a sip of her latte. "How does the parish hall look?" she asked.

"Nice. Well, it's still a cinder block box, basically, but the tables and tablecloths were all set up. The bouquet from the altar will go in the middle. I think they have some camellias to float in glass bowls here and there. And they had the punch bowl out. Not sure what's going to go in it. Maybe it's for the beer." Mary gave her an evil smile.

"Oh, please! I still have *no* idea what's going on with the food. Chase hasn't told me a thing. You didn't see any jumbo cans of Heinz baked beans in the kitchen, did you?"

"Nary a can. Stop worrying about that and start worrying about getting ready. Let's put our dresses on and see what we can do about your hair."

Laurie pulled her dress over her head and let her friend zip it. "It still looks gorgeous. I love it. Wait. Let me take a picture."

"I wish Lisa were here," Laurie said. Her sister and her father were flying in together, but the plane had been delayed. She had texted saying she was somewhere north of Redding, and would go straight to the church and get ready there. Their brother Mike would also be waiting at the church.

"That's what she gets for flying in the day of," Mary said. "I know, I know. Her mother-in-law's hip surgery and all the reasons." Mary placated Laurie who had started to protest. Lisa did seem to have good reasons for being late. "You'll have plenty of time to visit and commiserate after the ceremony."

Mary fixed Laurie's hair in the style they had practiced earlier in the week, a braided circlet around the crown of her head interwoven with a ribbon of crystal beads, and the rest of her hair flowing loosely down. "Perfect," Mary said as Laurie held up a mirror and tried to get a glimpse of the back.

Finally Laurie was ready and looking beautiful. Mary quickly slipped into her dress and shoes, and admired her reflection in the bathroom mirror. "Aren't you excited about finally moving into your new house?" she asked.

"I am stoked. I'm so happy with the way everything looks. Even the guitar wall, although it hurts to admit it, since I pitched such a fuss. I can't wait to wake up and go down to my beautiful kitchen and have coffee in that nice den with a fire in the fireplace, and look outside into the back yard. I won't miss this view of the pawnshop roof."

"All right, Ms. Lanton. Are you ready for me to drive you to the church?" Mary smiled. "I have to call you Ms. Lanton while I can, since you'll be Mrs. Harris in a couple of hours." She glanced at her watch. "Less than that! Good golly, we have to get moving!"

Mary drove and Laurie imprinted the scenery on her mind. It wasn't as if she was going to move far, but after today she would no longer make the daily drive from her apartment, across the railroad tracks and into the historic part of town. She felt a flutter of excitement in her stomach. She texted her sister one more time, and Lisa answered:

Waiting for you at the church. What's taking you?

"Thank God. My sister's already here."

The recent rain had brought out the green in the church lawn at St. Mark's. Cherry blossoms covered the small trees near the courtyard, and a few dog-wood blossoms were starting to show. "Park around back. We'll sneak in through the kitchen and hide out in the parlor. Chase said he was in Mother Barbara's office. I don't want him to see me."

"Okay." Mary parked, and the two took a quick look outside before exiting the car and dashing inside.

"Mary, there's no food in here," Laurie said as they walked quickly through the kitchen. There was a note of panic in her voice.

"Calm yourself, oh ye of little faith. I happen to know something you don't know."

"What?!" Laurie made an exasperated sound.

"Food will magically appear at the proper moment." There was a familiar, impish twinkle in Mary's eyes.

"You dirty dog. Wipe that little smile off your face."

Laurie forgot about food as she entered the parlor and greeted her siblings and her father. "You guys clean up nice," she said. "I'm so glad you made it."

"Well, it was hectic, but everything's going according to plan," Lisa said. Then she winked at Mike.

"Wait a minute. What's going on?" Laurie looked from Mary to Lisa, and at her brother Mike. "I have a feeling you guys have been up to something. You've been plotting against me."

Mary shrugged, looking clueless, but Mike stifled a laugh, and turned to Lisa. "Boy, that traffic was awful this morning wasn't it?"

"Oh, yes. The traffic was awful!" she said with an exaggerated nod.

"You guys!" Laurie stamped her foot. "What's going on?"

Her father said. "Has anyone noticed how beautiful you look today? That dress is very becoming."

Mary disappeared for a moment, and then returned with Laurie's bouquet. It felt cool after having spent the night in the flower room cooler. Laurie raised it to her nose and inhaled the delicate scent of fresh flowers. "Mary, do some reconnaissance and see who's out there."

Mary left and came back soon with a report. "Chase's brothers are all here. Everyone from the Treasure Chest. I noticed some people from the Coffee Pot. Scott and his wife are here. A bunch of guys who I guess must be Chase's crew from work. I'm not sure. And lots of regulars from church. Oh, and Sharon from the arts center. You're gonna be surprised. The church is about packed."

"Stand together. I need to get some pictures." Lisa pulled out her phone and started snapping, ordering people to assemble in various combinations.

"Give me that," Mary said, and snapped some pictures of Laurie with her sister. "Now I'm going to go join Pete. I'll see you after the ceremony."

Laurie had only a few more minutes to feel nervous before Mother Barbara came in. "There's still time, if you want to back out," she said, her head cocked with a smile.

"Nope." Laurie shook her head. "I've got my eyes wide open, and I'm going through with this."

"All righty then. Chase and I are heading through to the sanctuary. As soon as your family takes their seats you can join us and we'll get this show on the road."

Barbara pulled the door behind her. Lisa grabbed it before it shut completely, and watched through the crack. "We'll give them a minute to get out of the way," she said, and a moment later, "Okay. The coast is clear."

"Go out that way," Laurie indicated the side door leading outside from the office wing, "and we'll circle around to the front."

They walked around to the front of the church. The sun was just peeking out from the clouds. Laurie took it as a good omen. They entered the narthex together, and Mike and Lisa walked up the aisle of the nave to take their places in the first pew on the left, in front of Mary and Pete.

"I know we've been through this before," Laurie's dad said, "but as long as I live I'll be here to support you, even if it's from long distance. Will you let me walk you down the aisle again?"

Laurie hugged him tightly. "I'm glad you're here, Daddy," she said, grabbing a tissue from the box on the little table in the narthex. "But this time you're not 'giving me away.' I'm getting married to the man of my heart."

Laurie took her father's arm and the two stood at the back of the church. Steve had been noodling on the organ, but at a nod from Mother Barbara he burst into a joyful prelude. The congregation noted the change in music and turned in their seats, then rose as Laurie and her father started down the aisle.

Chapter 25.

Laurie was glad to have her father's arm to lean on. Her legs were suddenly rubbery and she felt awkward as she walked up the aisle with everyone watching. Briefly she imagined her mother looking on from her corner of heaven.

She swept her eyes from side to side, smiling at friends in the pews. The little church was full. Laurie was surprised so many people would take time away on a beautiful spring-like Saturday to celebrate with her and Chase.

Finally she allowed herself to look up the aisle at the groom, and a bubble rose in her throat. Chase wore a formal charcoal gray morning suit with a cutaway coat and a vest. His silvery paisley tie had champagne accents to coordinate with her dress. Laurie smiled broadly, and felt like she was looking in a mirror as Chase smiled back.

Lisa reached up to take the bouquet. Her father quietly placed Laurie's hand in Chase's, stepped away and took his seat. Laurie and Chase tore their eyes away from each other and faced Mother Barbara.

"Dearly beloved: We have come together in the presence of God to witness and bless the joining together of this man and this woman in holy matrimony," the priest began. "The bond and covenant of marriage ..."

Laurie's attention wandered as the priest continued on. Her eyes went to the flowers on the altar, lit by a beam of late-morning sunlight streaming in through the skylights high up in the ceiling. She shifted in her new shoes. She glanced at Chase, and at their hands clasped together; felt his thumb as he caressed the top of her hand, and heard him softly clear his throat. She gave his hand a squeeze.

"Into this holy union Laura May Lanton and Charles Wesley Harris now come to be joined." Laurie's attention shifted back to Mother Barbara as she heard her name spoken. "If any of you can show just cause why they may not lawfully be married, speak now; or else for ever hold your peace."

Laurie closed her eyes and held her breath for a long moment. The church was silent. She opened her eyes as Barbara commanded her attention.

"I require and charge you both, here in the presence of God, that if either of you know any reason why you may not be united in marriage lawfully, and in accordance with God's word, you do now confess it."

Laurie swallowed and looked at Chase, who appeared equally solemn. Then they both looked up at Barbara, who gently addressed Laurie.

"Laurie, will you have this man to be your husband; to live together in the covenant of marriage? Will you love him, comfort him, honor and keep him, in sickness and in health; and, forsaking all others, be faithful to him as long as you both shall live?"

"I will," she answered. She couldn't think of anything she wanted more.

The priest asked a similar question of Chase, and he answered in his clear, warm baritone, "I will." Laurie's heart fluttered. She reminded herself to breathe.

"Will all of you witnessing these promises do all in your power to uphold these two persons in their marriage?"

"We will" rang throughout the nave.

Laurie had reviewed the service over and over in the prayer book. Now certain phrases stood out as Mother Barbara proceeded at a stately pace. "Look mercifully upon this man and this woman who come to you seeking your blessing, and assist them with your grace, that with true fidelity and steadfast love they may honor and keep the promises and vows they make."

Laurie loved that word, "steadfast." The illustration of the steadfast tin soldier from a favorite children's book floated through Laurie's mind, and she glanced at Chase, standing straight beside her.

They sat, as friends from the congregation presented the scripture readings. Chase had teased Laurie with the idea of them singing the readings to each other, but in the end they opted for the easier way, and listened.

There was a reading from Colossians urging them to be compassionate and patient, to clothe themselves in love, and sing psalms with gratitude in their hearts.

Laurie smiled when psalm number one hundred twenty-eight was read next, comparing the wife to a fruitful vine around the house, and children like olive shoots around the table. Chase and Laurie were in agreement about having a family, and he winked at her when the lector read, "May you see your children's children."

They stood for the gospel reading, a selection from Matthew about being the salt and the light, and then sat beside each other again as Barbara moved to the lectern. She spoke briefly of all the changes she had observed in Chase and Laurie during the short year that she had known them. She talked about how giving they both were, and their contributions to their church and their community. Laurie felt her cheeks growing red.

Then the priest charged them to take the reading from Colossians to heart. "I can't say it any better than it was said in our readings today. 'Clothe yourselves with compassion, kindness, humility, meekness, and patience.'"

Chase leaned an inch closer to Laurie and whispered, "Church mouse." Laurie choked back a giggle.

"Bear with one another. Forgive each other," the priest continued.

Laurie said under her breath, "Guitar wall?"

"Let peace rule in your hearts, and be thankful."

Laurie was aware of Chase next to her, his hand clasped in hers, and the gratitude she felt in her heart.

Suddenly Chase stood, and Laurie sprang from her chair. They returned to their places in front of Mother Barbara, and the priest led Chase through the marriage vow. His voice was warm and resonant as always, but he made his vow to Laurie, and her alone as he took her right hand in his. "In the name of God, I, Charles, take you, Laura, to be my wife, to have and to hold from this day forward, for better for worse, for richer for poorer, in sickness and in health, to love and to cherish, until we are parted by death. This is my solemn vow."

Laurie then took his right hand, and Barbara led her through the vow. "In the name of God, I, Laura, take you, Charles." She stopped, blinking and swallowing. She squeezed her lips together tightly, willing herself not to cry.

"Deep breaths, Laurie, deep breaths," Barbara said quietly.

Laurie closed her eyes and breathed deeply. She opened her eyes and looked at Chase, his dark eyes solemnly gazing at her. "To be my husband, to have and to hold from this day forward, for better for worse, for richer for poorer, in sickness and in health, to love and to cherish, until we are parted by death. This is my solemn vow." She looked at his hand as she let go of it, and saw that it was red, she had squeezed it so hard. He flexed his fingers until the blood started to flow again.

Chase had brought their wedding bands to the altar earlier that morning. Now Barbara placed them on the open pages of her prayer book and blessed them. Chase took Laurie's ring in his right hand, and slid it into place on her ring finger. "Laura, I give you this ring as a symbol of my vow," he said, holding her hand. "And with all that I am," he paused to swallow. "And all that I have, I honor you, in the Name of God."

Laurie took his ring, placed it on his ring finger, and stood looking at it on his hand. Mother Barbara prompted her. "Charles, I give you this ring ..."

Laurie completed the sentence, looking at Chase, wondering at his loving smile.

Barbara joined Laurie and Chase's right hands together. "I pronounce that they are husband and wife."

It's done. We're married, Laurie thought, feeling stunned. The rest of the service went by in a blur.

As they knelt together Laurie tried to concentrate on the priest's words, remembering from her preparation how beautiful the prayers were. "Pour out the abundance of your blessing upon this man and this woman. Defend them from every enemy. Lead them into all peace. Let their love for each other be a seal upon their hearts, a mantle about their shoulders, and a crown upon their foreheads. Bless them in their work and in their companionship; in their sleeping and in their waking; in their joys and in their sorrows; in their life and in their death." Laurie squeezed Chase's hand. Then Barbara said loudly, "The peace of the Lord be always with you."

"And also with you," they replied automatically. They rose, and Chase took Laurie in his arms and gave her a long and lingering kiss.

A thundering recessional poured from the organ. Laurie looked up into the loft and laughed, as she saw Steve giving the keyboard a workout. Lisa pushed the bouquet into her hands with a whispered "congratulations," and Laurie floated down the aisle on Chase's arm and stepped out into the sunlight. They stood on the doorstep as members of the congregation flowed out behind them.

* * *

"Pictures! I need pictures." Lisa waved her cell phone over her head. The ushers directed guests to the parish hall as Chase and Laurie strolled arm in arm back to the altar. Those who were deemed necessary for the wedding album to come also obliged. Laurie's dad, Chase's brothers, Mother Barbara, and various friends and relatives were pressed into pictures in front of the altar. Then someone from the flower guild whisked away the great bouquet and carried it to the parish hall.

"Chase, I smell food and I've waited long enough. Can we go to our reception now?"

"You've been very patient. And you won't be disappointed." He let the rest of the party go ahead of them, and then led Laurie along the corridor and through the kitchen.

"Chase! What ...?" Laurie's mouth hung open as she waited for an explanation.

Bessie stood in the middle of the kitchen wearing her Tasty Chick apron and giving orders as Odette and Hazel bore beautifully-arranged platters of food into the hall.

"The insurance money and what the Treasure Chest gave us paid for fixing the building and buying most of the new equipment," Bessie said. "We just needed a little bit more to buy that new fryer. With the money from catering this wedding, the Tasty Chick should be re-opened before summer."

"Oh, Bessie I'm so glad!" Laurie and Bessie exchanged a hug.

"Honestly, I should have done it for nothing," Bessie said, "but that new husband of yours wouldn't let me!"

"Okay," Chase said pulling Laurie away. "Come on. I'm starved."

Looking over her shoulder, Laurie followed Chase into the parish hall. Music streamed from a speaker in the corner. The bouquet from the altar now sat at the center of the buffet, surrounded by platters full of delicate finger sandwiches of chicken salad and pimiento cheese, and heaping bowls of coleslaw and creamy potato salad. There were also golden cheese straws, miniature biscuits with honey, and platters of chicken fingers with sauces for dipping. The food looked beautiful, and smelled delicious. Laurie's mouth watered.

She looked for a place to set her bouquet, and saw the tiered white wedding cake on a table of its own. "Did Bessie make this too?"

"No. This is a gift from our friends at the Coffee Pot," Chase said.

Laurie laid her flowers on the table and studied the cake. The frosting swirls were actually eighth notes and exclamation points, and on top of the cake a miniature guitar leaned next to a folded newspaper. Laurie laughed out loud. "Perfect!" she said. "This is perfect."

The convivial crowd of well-wishers ate, drank, and mingled together, enjoying the reception. Chase's co-workers wasted no time loosening ties, many of which Laurie suspected had been purchased at the Treasure Chest especially for the event. She chatted and smiled her way around the hall as she and Chase accepted everyone's congratulations.

Finally Laurie squared her shoulders, took a deep breath, and walked over to greet Evelyn, who was standing behind the punch bowl serving cups of a frothy orange concoction.

"Chase's brothers are good looking, aren't they?" Evelyn said. "And tall!"

"But Chase is just the right height for me."

Evelyn extended a hand and lightly touched Laurie's arm. "Thank you again for the box you brought me. I can't tell you how much it means. I'm flying out to California in two weeks to visit Kim, my birth mother. I spent two hours on the phone with her last night." Her eyes shone with unshed tears.

As Laurie nodded at Evelyn her shoulders relaxed. She remembered Barbara's words, "Let peace rule in your hearts, and be thankful," and the last bit of tension and resentment drained from her body.

Chapter 26.

Guests wandered out to the church yard and gradually left the reception. Pete shook Chase's hand while Mary kissed Laurie on both cheeks. "Bye, Mrs. Harris. I wish you much happiness. Now get busy! I'm hoping little Ricky has a playmate by Christmas."

"I'll take your request under consideration," Laurie said. "No promises!"

Bessie and her crew packed up leftovers. Lisa urged Laurie and Chase out the door. "We'll deliver all this stuff and your wedding presents to your place, and then get out of there. We'll see you at church tomorrow."

Laurie stepped outside where Chase's pick-up truck was waiting, festooned with ribbons. Several strings of empty soda cans trailed from the back bumper. "Oh, no! Really?" she said.

"Hey, at least I was able to talk them out of filling the cab of the truck with shaving cream!" He helped her up into the seat, and they drove off, taking a long route through the middle of town and up and down some of the more historic avenues of Chinkapin. Finally they arrived at their home on Evergreen.

"The lights are on inside," Laurie said, her faced pressed to the truck's window. "Oh, doesn't it look homey and welcoming?"

Chase drove slowly past the front of the house and pulled into the driveway. The two held hands and strolled up the walk together. "Look, Chase. Lanterns on the front porch. And it says 'Welcome Home.' Is this Lisa's handiwork?" The bouquet from the parish hall was now on the table on the porch. Laurie pulled a small note off the welcome sign. "It says the food's in the fridge. How did she have time to do all of this?"

"She and your family did some of it yesterday evening. That's why I made sure you had your dress over at the apartment. You didn't think your sister really waited until the day of your wedding to fly down here, did you?"

"Did Mary know?"

"No. We were afraid she couldn't keep it a secret."

Chase unlocked the front door, slipped his keys into his pocket, and with one smooth motion lifted Laurie in his arms and carried her over the threshold. He set her gently down in the entryway where she could see the fire burning in the fireplace. "Oh, this is perfect," she said, as she kicked her shoes off and melted into her husband's arms.

They spent the afternoon in their wedding clothes relaxing in the living room. They opened gifts and envelopes, read all the cards together, and snacked on wedding cake and chicken salad sandwiches, enjoying their new home.

"Well, my bride, before I do any damage to this handsome, rented tux, I'd better take it off and hang it up. What do you say? Is it time to find out how comfortable our new bed is?"

Laurie kissed him on the lips and carried her shoes up the stairs. She went straight to her little boudoir, hung her pretty dress on the door of the armoire, and slipped into the peignoir she had bought at the Treasure Chest just before Valentine's Day. Then she stepped across the hall into her bedroom.

She could hear water running in the bathroom as she turned down the new bedsheets. She switched off all but a tiny bedside lamp, and padded nervously around the room in her bare feet, wondering at the butterflies in her stomach, since she had been intimate with Chase for months. She walked to the window and looked out into the deserted back yard, taking slow deep breaths, waiting for him to finish up.

She heard the water turn off, and the rattling of a door handle. On impulse, Laurie turned and drew the curtain across the window, hiding behind it as she held her breath.

"Laurie?" Chase's voice came from near the bedroom door. "I wonder where she could be. Maybe somewhere near those feet I see sticking out from under the curtain."

Busted, Laurie thought. With a swirl of fabric she turned to face the window. The soft sound of footsteps came closer. Her flesh tingled as she felt Chase behind her.

"What have I found?" he said, pressing his body against her and stroking her arms. The silky curtain glided smoothly over her satin peignoir. She leaned into him as he reached around her, sliding his hands over her hips and her belly, and making slow circles over her breasts.

Through the curtain she felt his breath warm on her neck. His body hardened as he reached lower to stroke her thighs, pulling her tightly to him. She was vaguely aware of moonlight bathing the yard as she looked out through lowered eyelids. Her breathing grew rapid and shallow.

Second Home

Chase pulled the curtain away, and as he had done earlier, he lifted her in his arms and laid her on the bed. Laurie reached for him as he bent over her. "I have one more wedding present to open," he said, and pulled gently at the satin ribbon over her breasts. The peignoir fell open, baring her soft skin in the moonlight.

* * *

"What is it? What's the matter?" Chase watched Laurie slip into her robe and slippers. "Did we miss the alarm?"

"No, it's still early. But I dreamed that we forgot to bring the coffee maker to our new house, and I was just going downstairs to see."

"And what would you do if your dream is real?" Chase said, grabbing her hand and pulling her back onto the bed.

"I would send you out to get one, dear husband," Laurie said. She leaned over and kissed him. "I love you, Mr. Harris."

"I love you back, Mrs. Harris. Now and forever. And you know, it's my job to make the coffee." He pulled on his robe and the two descended the stairs together.

"I *so* love my new kitchen!" Laurie said, looking out the windows into the yard as the coffee maker gurgled.

"You'll have to love it some more later. Now carry your coffee upstairs and start getting ready."

* * *

Side by side they walked across the church yard and up the stairs into the choir loft where Steve was warming up on the organ. Laurie took her seat and looked toward the altar, admiring the new bouquet the flower guild had placed there. She thought of her wedding flowers at home, and how lovely they had looked on her porch.

"Earth to Laurie. Come in, Laurie," Mary said, taking a seat beside her. "Gosh you look tired. Didn't you sleep last night?" she teased, with a glance back at Chase.

Laurie smiled, turning toward her. "Zip it, girlfriend. Actually our new bed was very comfy. You're joining us for brunch this morning, right?"

"Wouldn't miss it. Hopefully the little one will let us enjoy it."

Steve started the choir on vocal warm-ups. Then he asked them to turn to hymn 188. "We don't do this one often, so you may not recognize the tune. I'll play it through for you."

After listening a few moments Mary commented, "It sounds like something you would hear in a music box." She read the name of the tune at the bottom of the page. "Savannah. That's fitting, since now it looks like we're *both* Georgia peaches for good."

"And look, it's by Charles Wesley." Laurie turned and smiled at her lawfully-wedded husband.

"Okay, choir. Ready?" Steve played the last two measures by way of introduction. The choir lifted their voices and sang the hymn, which Laurie found very appropriate for the first day of her new life.

> *Love's redeeming work is done,*
> *Fought the fight, the battle won.*
> *Death in vain forbids him rise;*
> *Christ has opened paradise.*

THE END

ABOUT THE AUTHOR

Margaret Rodeheaver writes short fiction and novels for children and adults. She enjoys music, travel, and drinking coffee, and lives with her husband near Macon Georgia.

For information about Margaret Rodeheaver's latest books, sign up for email updates at www.MargaretRodeheaver.com

Writers Need Readers

Here are some ways you can support your favorite authors:

- Buy their books from your favorite retailer or online store.
- Ask your bookstore or library to stock their books.
- Write a review wherever you share information about books.
- Share or create a post about your favorite books on social media.
- Recommend books you enjoy to your friends or your book club. Word of mouth is still the number one way books are purchased.

Get acquainted with Chinkapin!

Hidden Treasure (Chinkapin series book 1)

Meet Laurie, who moves to Chinkapin from "up north" to get away from her ex, and her memories. She finds plenty to distract her in Chinkapin, including Chase, Jeff, a new job, and a home away from home at St. Mark's and the Treasure Chest Thrift Shop. Things get interesting when a real treasure is donated to the shop. But who is the creep, Chase or Jeff? And what do they both know that they aren't saying?

Finders Keepers (Chinkapin series book 2)

Laurie is sure of her heart, and she knows what she wants. So why all the suspicion when a couple of unfamiliar faces are seen around town? And why can't one of her co-workers at the thrift shop just dry up and blow away? Laurie chases a hunch, and her desire for a new home, across three counties, but it takes a new friend and an old one to help her see the truth.

Made in the USA
Middletown, DE
23 February 2023

25436332R00190